Tahiti

The Marriage of Loti

Set in Tahiti in 1872, this is an autobiographical novel that tells of the love affair between a beautiful island girl and the French naval officer who wrote under the name of Pierre Loti.

Pierre Loti, perhaps the world's most prolific, romantic and exotic travel writer and novelist, was born as Julien Marie Viaud in Rochefort in Western France in 1850. A childhood fascination with exotic lands across the seas led him to embark on a naval career that enabled him to seek love and adventure in many latitudes. He drew on these real life experiences when writing the romantic novels and travel books that made him one of the most popular authors of his day. Although his prolific output brought him both fame and fortune he remained a romantic escapist and never gave up his beloved naval career. He retired from the French navy in 1910 and died in 1923.

The Pierre Loti Library

Norman H. Hardy.

Tahiti

The Marriage of Loti

Pierre Loti

Routledge
Taylor & Francis Group

LONDON AND NEW YORK

First published in 2002 by
Kegan Paul Limited

This edition first published in 2011 by
Routledge
2 Park Square, Milton Park, Abingdon, Oxfordshire OX14 4RN

Simultaneously published in the USA and Canada
by Routledge
711 Third Avenue, New York, NY 10017

First issued in paperback 2016

Routledge is an imprint of the Taylor & Francis Group, an informa business

British Library Cataloguing in Publication Data
A catalogue record for this book is available from the British Library

ISBN 13: 978-1-138-98351-9 (pbk)
ISBN 13: 978-0-7103-0821-4 (hbk)

Publisher's Note
The publisher has gone to great lengths to ensure the quality of this reprint
but points out that some imperfections in the original copies may be
apparent. The publisher has made every effort to contact original copyright
holders and would welcome correspondence from those they have been
unable to trace.

ILLUSTRATIONS

"E hari te fau
E toro te faaro
E nau te taata."

The palm will grow,
The coral spread,
But man must die.

Old Polynesian saying.

INTRODUCTION

The Marriage of Loti – a tale of amorous dalliance set in Tahiti – is the exotic romance *par excellence*, one of the finest examples of that literary genre that enjoyed its European heyday between 1880 and 1914. These years saw the expansion of European colonial possessions abroad on an unprecedented scale, a development that was reflected in the emergence of a new kind of literature devoted to the colonial experience, and to life in all foreign lands beyond the seas. There were colonial adventures, travel books, military novels and memoirs, but the most popular form by far was the exotic romance, whose leading exponent was the French naval officer who wrote under the name Pierre Loti.

Loti's romances were a world away from the pallid pastiches in pasteboard settings favoured by his many imitators. Loti's forte was lyrical descriptive writing, and he also possessed an intimate knowledge of exotic people and places drawn from personal experience gained during naval service. The formula or his plots never varied, being composed of four basic elements; the action is set in a colourful foreign country, the lovers are a Western man and a woman native to the place, their affair is not conducted along Western lines but proceeds according to the customs of the country, and their relationship is temporary. In Loti's hands these simple elements were elaborated into compelling portrayals of the colonies as places where exciting adventures, exotic customs and erotic interludes were all to be found and enjoyed. Through the immense popularity of *The Marriage of Loti* and his other romances – among them *Madame Chrysanthemum*, the book that inspired Puccini's opera *Madame Butterfly* – Loti was responsible for establishing a romantic view of the colonies and the colonial experience in the mind of the public.

The Marriage of Loti was the romance that first won Loti a wide and enthusiastic following, and it contains some of the finest evocations of Polynesian settings ever written. Certainly Loti captures, as no other writer has, that atmosphere of melancholy – the dreamlike sense of isolation, of haunting sadness – that is familiar even today to all those who know the Pacific islands well. It is a work of the senses rather than of the intellect, a kind of literary impressionism that invites comparison with the paintings of Paul Gauguin, whose interest in the Pacific was fired by the book. In their separate ways, author and artist were responsible for fixing the romantic Polynesian idyll in the public imagination for all time. But while Gauguin's work is a vivid celebration and positive affirmation of the island way of life, *The Marriage of Loti* is of another complexion entirely, for it reveals the destructive aspect of the idyll and the dark side of the dream.

Julien-Marie Viaud, who later took the name Pierre Loti, was born in Rochefort in Western France in 1850. From earliest childhood, he was irresistably attracted to exotic lands. As he recalled;

> Oh! What magic and mental turmoil there was during my childhood in the simple word 'the colonies', which, at that time, denoted in my mind every far-off tropical land with its palm trees, enormous flowers, Negroes, animals and adventures . . . Oh, 'the colonies'! How can I describe everything that stirred in my head at the very sound of that word![1]

Polynesia – and Tahiti in particular – exerted a special fascination on the boy, inspired by the experiences of his older brother Gustave, a naval surgeon, who had been stationed in Tahiti for two years and had enjoyed a liaison with a Tahitian woman. Gustave died on service in Indochina when Julien was fifteen, but his Tahitian tales were not forgotten. Julien entered the French naval college at Brest with the aim of one day following his brother out to the colonies, and his voyage to the Pacific on the *Flore* when he was twenty-two was the realization, as he put it, of 'the dream of my entire childhood'.[2]

When the *Flore* arrived off Papeete on January 29, 1872, Julien found that the islands were a very different place to that 'earthly paradise' described by the French explorer Bougainville a century before. Congregationalist missionaries sent by the London Missionary Society had arrived in the islands in 1797, and within a few years had succeeded in destroying much of the traditional Tahitian way of life. Under their influence, observance of the great annual festivals was abandoned, the dancing of the *upa-upa* and singing of the ancient songs were forbidden, women were made to wear shapeless shifts over their *pareos* and men were forced to give up many of their customary sports and pastimes. By 1824, conditions in the islands were such that the Russian explorer Otto von Kotzebue was moved to observe:

> To pray and obey are the only commands laid upon an oppressed people . . . A police officer is specially appointed to enforce the prescribed attendance on the church and prayer meetings. I saw him in the exercise of his functions armed with a bamboo cane, driving his herd to the spiritual pasture . . . It is true that the religion of the missionaries has, with a great deal of evil, effected some good . . . It has restrained the vices of theft and incontinence, but it has given birth to bigotry, hypocrisy, and a hatred and contempt for all other modes of faith.[3]

This bigotry proved to be the undoing of the Congregationalist hegemony in Tahiti. On their advice, the young Queen Pomare IV expelled two French Roman Catholic priests from the islands in 1837, an incident that led to a punitive visit by the French admiral Dupetit-Thouars in 1838, and finally resulted in the Queen's being forced to accept the establishment of a French protectorate over Tahiti – events that are vividly described by Herman Melville in *Omoo*. By 1872, Tahiti was a colony of

France in all but name, Pomare IV was a Queen in name only, and the once proud and vigorous Tahitian people were suffering from the physical, social and spiritual maladies that betoken a culture in decline and distress. It is therefore not surprising that Julien's first impressions of Tahiti were disappointing, and *The Marriage of Loti* begins on this note;

> If this land of dreams was to remain the same for me I ought never to have laid my finger on it . . . And civilization, too, has been overbusy; our hateful colonial civilization, with our conventionality, our habits and vices; and wild poetry flees away with the customs and traditions of the past.[4]

The 'baptism' that opens the book and marks the entree of Harry Grant into Tahitian society also marks the transformation – both literal and literary – of Julien Viaud into Loti. It was in Tahiti that Loti first devised and embarked upon the approach he would in future use to acquaint himself with other cultures – by living as much among the people as his naval duties would allow, by learning their language, dressing in their fashion and loving their women, recording his experiences in diaries that would later become sources for his novels. While Loti's prose is highly imaginative, his plots are not. All of the major characters in *The Marriage of Loti* are based on known people; the members of Pomare's court are historical figures, Harry Grant is based on Julien Viaud, Plunkett on his shipmate Lucien Hervé Jousselin,[5] George or Rouéri on Julien's brother Gustave, Taïmaha on Gustave's mistress Tarahu, and while the girl Rarahu is known to be a composite of several Tahitian women she, too, may be regarded as real and is not, as was Melville's Fayaway in *Typee*, a child of the author's imagination. In its broad outlines, the storyline also parallels known facts of the author's life – the hero follows a much loved dead brother to the islands, seeks out his brother's former mistress, enjoys amorous dalliances of his own, establishes a temporary menage and finally sails away. As for the thoughts, actions and emotions attributed to the hero, they are revealed by the diaries to correspond to those of the author at the time the events took place. While Loti edited, embellished and manipulated material for dramatic effect when writing his novels, *The Marriage of Loti* may nonetheless be considered to be substantially a work of fact, rather than of pure fiction. The book must therefore be taken on two levels; as a literary work, and as an account of one man's true life experiences in Tahiti in the early 1870s. Seen in this way, *The Marriage of Loti* is a contradictory, complex and disturbing account, in which the literary talents of Loti the author ultimately tell against the attitudes and actions of Loti the man.

Loti's early misgivings about the islands are soon swept aside. As he puts it;

> I, too, am under the spell – the wonderful charm of this country, so unlike every other. I fancy I see it now as George used to see it, through the same transfiguring prism. It is already two months since I first set foot on the island, and already I am bewitched. The disappointment of the first few days is now a thing of the past . . . .[6]

For the hero of the book, as his brother before him, the transfiguring prism that makes him see the islands in a new light is love.

Although Loti's liaison with Rarahu continues throughout the book, its character does not change from start to finish. Significantly, Loti's role throughout is a passive one – he does not initiate the affair, but merely allows himself to give in, both to the girl's affection for him and, later, to the suggestion that they enter into a temporary 'marriage'. Having accepted the girl's love, he quickly comes to accept what he believes to be her view of him and of their relative positions;

> She never thought of herself as being in Loti's eyes – child of fifteen as she was – anything more than a strange little being, a plaything for a time, soon to be forgotten.[7]

Although he protests that his feeling for her is 'of a less vulgar stamp', he does nothing to prove it, and is content for Rarahu to love him' '. . . as we love some supernatural being whom we can scarcely grasp or comprehend'.[8] But having accepted Rarahu's love, Loti is dismissive of any hopes she may entertain for future;

> Loti, though dressed as a Tahitian and speaking her language, was still to her a *Paoupa* – that is to say, one of the men who come from the impossible lands beyond the ocean . . . Then too, she knew that Loti would soon go away, never to return . . .[9]

The parameters of the affair are now set. Because Loti has not taken the active role in initiating the liaison, he apparently feels justified in refusing to accept responsibility for the consequences of his actions. He agrees with Rarahu's conception of him as a superior being; therefore, their relationship cannot be that of equals. Because he accepts – as she in fact does not – that he is bound to leave her, their affair can never be permanent. So although the relationship may continue for some time, it can never develop.

The Marriage of Loti[10] was published in 1880, to acclaim from critics and public alike. *Le Figaro*[11] described it as 'one of the most charming works to have appeared for a long time', *Le Temps* found it 'charming, new without extravagance, original without affectation'[12] and *Le Siècle* pronounced that;

> (in addition to) . . . the charm of style . . . It is also the turnings of the spirit of the author, the mixture of tender gaiety and true sensibility that gives to events that he recounts a particular physiognomy . . . there reigns a freshness of sentiment, a soft melancholy and a poetic charm that sets it apart.[13]

As for the public, the novel's 'voluptuous dream-like quality stole over the materialistic French readers like some insidious spell',[14] and its popularity was such that the book quickly ran to several editions.

Loti's charming style and lyrical prose were not the only factors behind the phenomenal success of *The Marriage of Loti* and his other exotic romances, for their appeal was in large part due to their accurate reflection of the attitudes to the colonies that prevailed in his day. The passage of time and a changed political climate have prompted some modern scholars to take a harsh approach to the books that were received so uncritically when they first appeared. In their view, Loti's writings were a form of *literary imperialism* that promoted notions of racial superiority and justified 'Europe's civilizing mission vis a vis the lower races'[15] of the world;

> . . . Loti owes his popularity in part to the romantic fantasies of personal glory and amorous success in which he enabled his readers to indulge. More generally, Loti's works help to sustain gratifying images of cultural superiority among his European readers. To enjoy reading Loti is to enjoy the personal and cultural complacency on which the colonial venture thrived.[16]

After the publication of *The Marriage of Loti*, Loti continued to pursue a dual career as naval officer and author, writing thirty-nine books and many short stories and articles before he died in 1923. At the end of *The Marriage of Loti*, the hero reflects that Tahiti;

> . . . is a delightful land when one is but twenty; but one soon gets tired of it, and perhaps it is as well not to go back after one has turned thirty.[17]

Loti took his own advice, and never returned to the islands after his visit on the *Flore*. But twenty-six years later, 1898, his memories were revived when he attended a performance of *L'Ile du Rêve*, Reynaldo Hahn's musical version of *Le Marriage of Loti*. Loti found the performance deeply moving;

Then I shut my eyes to see myself once more – oh! to see again – with what inexpressible sadness – the true scene . . . over there, across how many seas, far far away in the depth of time past . . . and it was as if under layer upon layer of ashes I found again the faces, the scents and that marvellous intoxication of my youth, in that vanished midnight, among the orange trees, under the southern stars . . .[18]

Kaori O'Connor

NOTES

1 From Loti's *Le Roman d'un Enfant*, p 71–2. In Hargreaves, Alec G.: *The Colonial Experience in French Fiction*. Macmillan, London, 1981: p 23.
2 From Loti's *Un Jeune Officier Pauvre*, p 36. In Serban, N.: *Pierre Loti, Sa Vie et Son Oeuvre*. Les Presses Francaises, Paris, 1924: p 40.
3 Haldane, Charlotte: *Tempest Over Tahiti*. Constable, London, 1963; p 41.
4 Loti, Pierre: Tahiti: *The Marriage of Loti*. KPI, London & New York, 1986: p 15.
5 Blanch, Lesley: *Pierre Loti, Portrait of an Escapist*. Collins, London, 1983: p 63.
6 Loti, ibid: p 37–8.
7 ibid: p 58.
8 ibid: p 130.
9 ibid: pp 57–8.
10 *The Marriage of Loti* was first published under the title *Rarahu*.
11 Serban, ibid: p 249.
12 ibid: p 249.
13 ibid: pp 249–250.
14 Blanch, ibid: p 144.
15 Hargreaves, ibid: p 37.
16 ibid: p 84.
17 Loti, ibid: p 214–5.
18 Blanch, ibid: p 240.

PART I

The Marriage of Loti

I

BY LOTI'S FRIEND PLUNKET

LOTI was baptized on the 25th of January, 1872, at the age of twenty-two years and eleven days. When the deed was done, it was about one in the afternoon by London and Paris time. On the other side, and the other way up of the terrestrial ball, in the gardens of Queen Pomaré, where the event took place, it was near midnight. In Europe it was a cold and dismal winter's day. On the other side, in the queen's gardens, it was a calm, languorous, enervating summer's night.

Five persons took part in this ceremony of baptism amidst mimosas and orange-trees, in a fervid and fragrant air, under a sky starry with southern constellations. These five were Ariitéa, princess of the blood, Faïmana and Téria, ladies in attendance on her majesty, Plunket and Loti, midshipmen in the royal navy of Great Britain. Loti, who had hitherto been known as Harry Grant, still kept that name in all official documents and on the books of the ship he was attached to; but that of Loti was commonly adopted among his friends.

The ceremony was simple and performed without much speech or paraphernalia. The three Tahitian girls, who wore crowns of natural flowers and tunics of pink muslin with long skirts, after vainly endeavouring to pronounce such barbarous words as Harry Grant and Plunket—their Polynesian throats finding the harsh consonants impossible,—determined to know the youths by the names of Rémuna and Loti,* being those of two flowers. Next morning all the court was informed of this decision, and Harry Grant had no further existence in Oceania, any more than his friend Plunket.

It was furthermore agreed that the first words of a native song : " Loti taimané, etc."—sung discreetly and warily at night in the neighbourhood of the palace, should be understood to convey " ' Rémuna is here,' or ' Loti is here,' or both of them; and they beg their fair friends to come out at their call, or at least to come noiselessly and open the garden gate."

.   .   .   .

II

A BIOGRAPHICAL NOTE ON RARAHU; PLUNKET'S

REMINISCENCES

Rarahu was born in January, 1858, in the island or Bora-Bora, in 16° south latitude and 154° west longitude. At the moment when this tale begins she had just completed her fourteenth year.

* The author's orthography of Polynesian names and words has been retained in this translation.

She was a very strange little person, whose startling and savage charm was a thing quite apart from all the conventional rules of beauty recognized by the nations of Europe. While very young, her mother had sent her away in a long canoe with sails which was making for Tahiti. She remembered nothing of her native island but the enormous and terrible central tor which towers up from it. The profile of that gigantic block of basalt, rising like a stupendous corner-stone from the bosom of the Pacific, remained in her mind as the only image of her native land. Rarahu recognized it at a later day with mingled emotions, drawn in Loti's sketch-book, and this incident was in the first instance what roused her great love for him.

III

Rarahu's mother had brought her to Tahiti, the big island, the queen's island, to make a present of her to a very old woman of the Apiré district to whom she was distantly related. This was in obedience to an ancient custom of the Tahitian race by which children rarely grow up in the care of their mother. Adoptive fathers and mothers (faa amu) are there most common, and the family is collected as chance directs. This time-honoured exchanging of children is one of the quaint peculiarities of Polynesian manners.

IV

HARRY GRANT (LOTI, BEFORE HE WAS RENAMED) TO
HIS SISTER AT BRIGHTBURY, YORKSHIRE
(ENGLAND)

TAHITI ROADS, *January* 20, 1872.

" My dear Sister: Here I am, in sight of the distant isle which our brother loved so well, the mysterious speck of land which was for so long the scene of my childish dreams. A strange longing to come here contributed in no small degree to prompt me to adopt a seaman's life—of which I am already sick and tired.

" Years have gone by and made a man of me. I have been almost all over the world, and at last I behold the island of my dreams. But I have found nothing but melancholy and bitter disappointment.

" And yet it is verily and indeed Papeete; there is the queen's palace, over there among the greenery, the bay shaded by palms, the mountains beyond with their jagged outline—it is all just as I knew it would be. I have seen it all any time these ten years in the sketches George sent home, yellow with the sea and made poetical by distance; it is the very spot of earth of which the brother we have lost would talk so fondly.—Yes, all that, but minus the charm, the wondrous charm of vague illusions, of childhood's strange and fantastic impressions.—Dear me! yes, an island, like any other; and I, Harry, gazing at it, the self-same Harry as at Brightbury or London or where you will; so much the same that I do not believe I have even travelled hither.

" Ah ! if this land of dreams was to remain the same to me I ought never to have laid my finger on it.

" Besides, the fellows on board have spoiled my Tahiti, by picturing it from their point of view. Go where they will they can never escape from their commonplace selves; they smear all that is poetical with their slime of mockery, their own dulness and ineptitude. And civilization, too, has been overbusy; our hateful colonial civilization, with our conventionality, our habits and vices; and wild poetry flees away with the customs and traditions of the past.

.   .   .   .

" In short, during these days since the *Reindeer* cast anchor off Papeete, your brother Harry has remained on board, his spirit crushed and his fancy cheated.   .   .   .   .

.   .   .   .

" As for John, he is not like me, and I believe he is charmed with this place; since we arrived I have hardly seen him. He is still the same faithful and unfailing friend, the kind and loving brother who watches over me like a guardian angel and whom I love most truly with all my heart.   .   .   .

.   .   .   .

V

Rarahu was a little creature unlike any one else, though she was a perfect specimen of the Maori race which has peopled the Polynesian archipelagos, and which is one of the finest types of humanity. A very distinct race, too, whose origin and birthplace remain an unsolved mystery.

Rarahu's eyes were of a tawny black, full of exotic languor and coaxing softness, like those of a kitten when it is stroked; her eyelashes so long and so black that you might have taken them for painted feathers. Her nose was short and delicate, like the nose in some Arab faces; her mouth, rather too thick and too wide for a classic model, had deep corners deliciously dimpled. When she laughed she showed all her teeth, somewhat large teeth of brilliantly white enamel, not yet polished by the wear of years but showing the striations of young growth. Her hair, scented with sandal-wood oil, was long, straight and rather harsh, falling in heavy locks on her bare shoulders. Her skin was of the same hue all over, from her forehead to the tips of her toes; a dusky brown, verging on brick-red, like that of old Etruscan terra-cotta pottery. Rarahu was small, beautiful in proportion and mould; her bosom was purely formed and polished; her arms as perfect as an antique. Round her ankles a pattern was tattooed blue to imitate anklets; across her lower lip were three faint blue lines like those of the women of the Marquesas; and on her forehead a still paler outline of tattoo suggested a coronet. The feature most characteristic of her race was the small space between her eyes which like the eyes of all Maoris were by no means deep-set. When she was laughing and gay this gave her face the mischievous shyness of a marmoset; when she was grave or sad, there was some-

thing about her which can only be described as
Polynesian grace.

VI

Queen Pomaré's court was decked for a small
reception on the day when I first set foot on the soil
of Tahiti. The English admiral in command of the
Reindeer was to pay his respects to her majesty on
his arrival—she was an old acquaintance of his—
and I, in full uniform, was his escort.

The thick foliage overhead screened us from the
scorching sun of two in the afternoon; the shady
avenues which constitute Papeete, the queen's
capital, were silent and deserted. The huts with
verandahs, scattered among the tall trees in the
gardens and great tropical shrubs seemed, like the
inhabitants, to be sunk in the luxurious slumber of
the siesta. Close to the palace even all was still and
peaceful.

One of the queen's sons, a tawny colossus, in
evening dress, who came to meet us, led us into a
drawing-room with closed shutters where a dozen
women were sitting, all silent and motionless. In
the middle of the room stood two large gilt arm-
chairs, side by side. Pomaré, who was sitting in
one, desired the admiral to be seated in the other,
while an interpreter transmitted official compliments
between the old friends.

This woman, whose name had so long figured in
the exotic dreams of my childhood, I now beheld
in the flesh, dressed in a long garment of rose-
coloured silk, with the features of an old copper-

coloured woman, stern and imperious-looking. In the massive ugliness of her old age I could still trace what might have lent her in youth the attractions and prestige of which the navigators of a past time have left a record. The women who attended her, in this twilight of shade and the stilly calm of a tropical day, had an indefinable charm. They were almost all handsome in the Tahitian style of beauty : black eyes, languishing looks, and the dusky amber hue of the Gitanos. Their hair, falling loosely, was decked with natural flowers, and their long gauzy dresses, unconfined at the waist, fell to their feet in straight flowing folds.

My eyes rested more especially on the Princess Ariitéa;—Ariitéa with her sweet, pensive, dreamy face, and pale roses twined here and there in her black tresses.

VII

The first civilities having been exchanged, the admiral said to the queen: " This is Harry Grant, whom I wish to present to your majesty. He is a brother of George Grant, an officer in our navy, who lived for four years in your beautiful country."

The interpreter had scarcely finished the sentence when Queen Pomaré held out her wrinkled hand to me; a bright frank smile—no official grimace, lighted up her old face. " Rouéri's brother ! " said she, giving him his Tahitian name. " You must come and see me again." And she added in English : " Welcome ! " which it would seem was a special mark of favour as the queen never speaks any but her native language.

" Welcome ! " said the Queen of Bora-Bora likewise, displaying her large cannibal teeth in a broad smile. And I went away delighted with this strange court.

VIII

Rarahu, from her earliest infancy had scarcely ever left the cabin inhabited by her old adoptive mother, who lived in the Apiré district by the brook Fataoua.

Her business in life was very simple : to dream, to bathe—especially to bathe—to sing, and to wander through the woods with Tiahoui, her inseparable companion. Rarahu and Tiahoui were a pair of careless, laughing little beings, living almost entirely in the waters of their brook where they leaped and sported like a couple of flying-fish.

IX

It must not, however, be supposed that Rarahu was wholly unlearned; she could read her Tahitian Bible, and write in a large and very firm hand, the soft words of her native tongue; nay, she was strong in spelling by the rules of orthography as laid down by the brothers Picpus, who constructed a conventional code of syllables in the Latin character to represent Polynesian sounds. Many a child in our own fields is certainly less well-educated than this little savage maid. But it cannot have cost her any great pains at the missionary school at Papeete, for she was utterly idle by nature.

X

After following the road to Apiré for about half an hour, if you turn to the right through the thicket you come to a wide natural basin hollowed out of the living rock. Into this pool the Fataoua falls in a cascade of swift waters of delicious freshness.

There all day there was company to be found; the beauties of Papeete, stretched on the grass, and spending the tropical days in chattering, singing and sleeping, or else in swimming and diving like lively gold-fish. They plunged in dressed in their muslin gowns and kept them on, all wet as they were, to go to sleep as the Naiads did of old.

Thither seamen, on shore for a few hours, would come to take their pleasure; there the black witch Tétouara reigned over the revels; there, in the shade, was there much eating of oranges and guavas.

Tétouara was a black woman of the Kanack race of Melanesians. A ship coming from Europe had picked her up one day, a thousand leagues away, in an island near New Caledonia, and had dropped her at Papeete where she produced much the same effect as a woman from Congo might among a bevy of English misses. Tétouara with her inexhaustible good humour, monkey-like high spirits, and absolute immodesty, kept all about her gay and stirring. This peculiarity made her invaluable to her indolent companions; she was a prominent figure at the falls of Fataoua.

XI

It was about noon, on a calm and scorching day, when first I saw my little friend Rarahu. The young Tahitian women who frequented the Falls, drowsy with the heat, were lying on the grassy bank close to the stream, their feet dipping in the clear cool water. The same green shade lay over us, vertical and motionless; large black velvet butterflies marked with lavender eyes fluttered languidly past, or rested on us, as though their sheeny wings were too heavy to bear them; the air was charged with heady and unfamiliar perfume; quite unconsciously I abandoned myself to this enervating existence, overborne by the Oceanian spell.

The undergrowth of mimosa and guava-trees in the background of the picture, was suddenly parted; there was a gentle rustle of leaves, and two little girls peered forth studying the situation like two mice peeping out of a hole. They were crowned with head-dresses of leaves to shelter their heads from the heat of the sun; they were girt with *pareos* (loin-cloths) of dark blue with broad yellow stripes; their slender dusky bodies were otherwise bare; their long black hair hung loose.—No Europeans to be seen, nothing to scare them. The two children, feeling quite safe, stole out to lie under the waterfall which tumbled and splashed noisily about them. The prettier of the two was Rarahu; the other was Tiahoui, her friend and confidante.

Then Tétouara, roughly seizing my arm, my navy blue sleeve with its gold braiding, held it up high above the long grass in which I was lying, and displayed it to them with an indescribable twinkle of mischievous fun, shaking it like a scarecrow.

The two little things, startled like two birds who catch sight of a baboon, fled in a panic—and that was our introduction, our first interview.

XII

The information which Tétouara forthwith volunteered came to this:

" They are a pair of little simpletons, not like the others; they will never do anything like other people. Old Huamahine, who has the care of them, is a woman with principles, and forbids their having anything to do with us."

Tétouara, for her part, would have been only too glad if I could have tamed these little wild birds, and she strongly urged me to make the attempt.

To overtake them I need only, as she said, follow an almost invisible track through the guava-grove which would bring me to another pool about a hundred paces off, lying higher up the stream, and less frequented. " There," she said, " the waters of the Fataoua fill another rock-basin made on purpose, one might say, for the meetings of two or three intimate friends. It was the private bath of Rarahu and Tiahoui; their childhood had been spent there as one might say. . . ."

It was a retired nook, vaulted over by tall bread-fruit trees with their thick leaves, enclosed by acacias, guavas, and sensitive plants. The cool water danced noisily over the small polished pebbles, and a murmur from the lower basin came up from a distance, with the laughter of women and Tétouara's shrill tones.

XIII

.   .   .   .

". . . Loti," said Queen Pomaré a month later, in her big, hoarse voice, " Loti, why should you not marry little Rarahu of Apiré? It would be far better, I assure you, and would do you good among the people."

We were under the verandah of the palace when the question was put to me. I was lying at full-length on a mat and held five cards which had just been dealt to me by my friend Téria; before me reclined my singular adversary in the game—the queen, who had a perfect passion for écarté. She had on a wrapper of yellow stuff flowered with black, and was smoking a long pandanus cigarette made of a single leaf rolled up. Two ladies-in-waiting shuffled the cards and helped us with their advice, looking eagerly over our shoulders.

Outside, the rain was falling, the warm-scented torrent which comes with the summer tempests in those latitudes; the plumy leaves of the coco-palms bent under the deluge, their strong ribs streaming

with water. The clouds piled above the hills made
a terribly dark and gloomy background, and at the
very top of the weird scene towered the black peak
of Fataoua. The atmosphere was saturated with
the stormy exhalations which excite the senses and
the fancy.

.   .   .   .

"Marry little Rarahu of Apiré!" The suggestion was unexpected. I must think it over.

.   .   .   .

I need hardly say that the queen, who was a very
judicious and sensible woman, did not mean a
marriage according to European laws, a bond for
life. She was very indulgent to the manners and
customs of her people, though she often did her best
to reform them and bring them into closer con-
formity with Christian principles. It was only a
Tahitian marriage which she proposed to me. I had
no very real motive for resisting her majesty's wish,
and little Rarahu of Apiré was a sweet person.

However, with no small embarrassment, I pleaded
my youth. I was, besides, in some sort, under the
guardianship of the admiral on board the *Reindeer*,
and he might regard such an union with no favour-
able eye.—And then marriage is an expensive business, even in Oceania.—And moreover—and above
all—we must ere long be sailing, and the inevitable
consequence would be leaving Rarahu in tears, a
very cruel end.

Pomaré smiled at all my reasoning, which by no

means convinced her. After a moment's silence she offered me Faïmana, her lady-in-waiting, and this time I refused point-blank. Then her face assumed an expression of keen amusement, and her eyes gently turned on Ariitéa the princess. "If I had offered her," said she, "perhaps you would have accepted more readily, my little Loti?"

The old woman revealed by this speech that she had guessed the third, and certainly the most serious of my heart's secrets.

Ariitéa dropped her eyes and a faint rosy glow spread over the dusky amber of her cheeks; I myself felt the blood rushing to my face, and the thunder began to mutter in the bowels of the mountains, like an ominous orchestra emphasizing the critical point of a melodrama.

Pomaré, well pleased with her own little jest, laughed in her sleeve. She had taken advantage of the disturbance she had occasioned to mark *té tâné* (the man)—that is to say, the king—twice over. Pomaré, with whom écarté was a favourite pastime, was a determined cheat; she would cheat even at a public reception in the games she played with admirals in port, or the governor, and the few gold pieces she might win certainly counted for nothing in the pleasure she felt in beating her adversary.

XIV

Rarahu possessed two muslin frocks, one pink and the other white, which she wore alternately on

Sundays, over her blue and yellow *pareo,* to go to the Protestant missionary church at Papeete. On those occasions her hair was divided into two long and very thick black plaits, and over one ear, where an old scrivener sticks his pen, she stuck a large hibiscus flower, whose vivid red contrasted with the paleness of her coppery cheek.

She never lingered in Papeete after service was over, but avoided the society of other young women and the booths of the Chinese vendors of tea, cakes, and beer. She was very well-behaved, and hand in hand with Tiahoui she went back to Apiré to take off her finery. A little suppressed smile and a glance of recognition were the only sign of understanding I ever got from the two damsels when by chance we met in the avenues near Papeete.

XV

We had already spent many hours together, Rarahu and I, on the bank of the Fataoua river, when Pomaré made the startling suggestion that we should be married. And Pomaré, who knew everything she cared to know, knew that perfectly well. I had hesitated a long time. I had rebelled with all my might—and this strange state of things had gone on beyond all reason for several days; when we lay down for our noonday nap on the grass, Rarahu with her arms round me, we went to sleep side by side for the world like two brothers. It was a purely childish comedy that we played together, and very certainly no one would have suspected it. That the feeling "which gave Faust pause at Margaret's door" should come between me and a Tahitian girl, would have made me smile perhaps a few years later; it would at any rate have been a very good joke in the captain's room on board the *Reindeer,* and would have made me supremely ridiculous in the eyes of Tétouara.

.   .   .   .

Rarahu's old foster-parents, whom I at first feared to grieve, had ideas on such subjects which are not current in Europe, and I was not slow to discover this. They said that a great girl of fourteen was no longer a child, and was not created to live alone. She did not walk the streets of Papeete and that was all they asked of her propriety. They thought Loti better than many another—Loti who, like her, was young, who seemed gentle-tempered and appeared to be fond of her—so after due reflection the old folks approved.

And even John, my good brother John, who looked on the world about him with such astounding purity of vision, and who was distressed and surprised when he heard of my wanderings at night with Faïmana, in the queen's gardens—John, I say, was indulgent to the little girl, who had quite charmed him. He liked her childlike candour, and her great affection for me; he was ready to forgive his brother Harry if she was in the case.

XVI

PALACE AFFAIRS

Ariifaité, the prince-consort, played an almost invisible part at the court of his queen. Pomaré, whose aim it was to give the Tahitians a royal family of vigorous mould, had chosen this man as being the tallest and handsomest to be found in her island-realm. He was still a splendid old man, with white hair, a majestic figure, and noble and regular features. But he would not be presentable, obstinately refusing to wear enough clothes; the simple loin-cloth of his country to him seemed sufficient, and he never could accustom himself to a dress-coat. Moreover he often got drunk, so on the whole he was rarely on show.

The children of this marriage were a race of giants, who all died of the same incurable disease, like those great tropical giants which make all their growth in a season and perish in the autumn. They all died of lung-disease, and the queen watched them go before her, one after another, with a grief beyond words. The eldest, Tamatoa, married to the beautiful Moé, had one exquisitely pretty child, Princess Pomaré V., the heiress presumptive to the throne, idolized by her grandmother, the old queen, Pomaré IV. This little girl, who in 1872 was six years old, already betrayed signs of the hereditary malady, and more than once I had seen the grandmother's eyes fill with tears as they fell on her. This anticipated doom to certain death lent an added charm to this little creature, the last of the race of Pomaré, the last of the queens of the Tahitian archipelago. She was as bewitching and as capricious as a little invalid princess can be when she is never crossed in anything. The affection she had conceived for me recommended me to the queen.

XVII

In order to be able to talk to Rarahu in her own tongue, to understand all her thoughts, even the deepest or the strangest, I made up my mind to learn Maori. To this end I one day purchased at Papeete the dictionary compiled by the brothers Picpus, a little old book of which but one edition was ever printed, and of which a few rare copies are scarcely to be met with at all now. This book was what first opened to me strange views of Polynesia—an un-explored field for reverie and study.

XVIII

At first I was struck by the vast number of mystical words derived from the old Maori religion, and then by the multitude of sad, weird, untranslatable words which on those shores express the vague terrors of the darkness, the mysterious utterances of nature, the scarcely articulate stirrings of the fancy.

First there was *Taaroa*, the supreme divinity of the Polynesian mythology.   Then the goddesses:

Ruahine tahua, the goddess of the arts, and of prayer.

Ruahine auna, the goddess of anxious care.

Ruahine faaipu, the goddess of sincerity.

Ruahine Nihonihororoa, the goddess of quarrelling and murder.

Romatane, the priest who admits souls to heaven, or who excludes them.

Tutahoroa, the way by which souls depart to eternal night.

Tapaparaharaha, the base on which the world rests.

Ihohoa, departed spirits, ghosts.

Oroimatua, ai aru nihonihororoa, a dead body, a vampire, which comes to life again to devour the living.

Tuitupapau, a prayer to the dead not to revisit the earth.

Tahurere, a prayer to a dead friend to injure a living enemy.

Tii, a malignant spirit.

Tahutahu, a magician or sorcerer.

Mahoi, the essence or soul of a god.

Faa-fano, the departure of the soul at death.

Ao, the world, universe, earth, sky, happiness, paradise—a cloud, light, element—the centre or heart of things.

Po, night, the ancient past, an unknown dark world, hell.

And then such words as these, taken as they come from among a thousand :

Moana, the depths of the sea or the sky.

Tohureva, the presentiment of death.

Natuaea, a confused or illusory vision.

Nupa nupa, darkness, bewilderment.

Ruma-ruma, darkness, melancholy.

Tarehua, to be dull-witted, or visionary (second sight).

Tataraio, to be bewitched.

Tunoo, malignancy.

Ohiohio, the evil eye.

Puhiairoto, a secret foe.

Totoro ai po, a mysterious banquet in the darkness.

Tetea, a pale face, a phantom.

Oromatua, the skull of a relation.

Papaora, the smell of the dead.

Tai hitoa, a terrific voice.

Tai aru, a voice like the surf.

Tururu, a trumpeting to rouse fear.

Oniania, giddiness, the wind rising.

Tape tape, the line where the sea grows deep.

Tahau, to whiten anything in the dew.

Rauhurupe, an old banana-tree; a decrepit person.

Tutai, red clouds on the horizon.

Nina, to get rid of a sad thought. To bury.

Ata, a cloud, the stem of a flower, a messenger, the twilight.

Ari, depth, emptiness; a wave of the sea.

XIX

Rarahu was possessed of a cat of a hideous kind, in whom all her affections were centred till my arrival. Cats are an object of luxury in Oceania, and yet the breed there is utterly degenerate. Imported cats introduce new blood, and a cat of good strain is highly prized. Rarahu's cat was a great lean beast, very long in the shanks, which spent all its time asleep warming itself in the sun, or eating blue land-crabs. It was called Turiri. Its erect ears were pierced at the tips, and ornamented with little silk tassels after the fashion of cats in Tahiti. This headgear gave the finishing-touch of comicality to the cat's face, which was strange enough in itself. Turiri even dared to follow its mistress to the bathing-place, and would spend hours with us, sprawling in luxurious attitudes. Rarahu would lavish the fondest names on this creature, such as : " my darling little thing," or " my little heart," (ta ú mea iti here rahi) and (ta ú mafatu iti).

XX

. . . .

. . . No. Those who have lived only in the midst of the half-civilized hussies of Papeete, who have learned from them only the easy mongrel Tahitian which is spoken on the beach, only the ways and manners of the colonized town—those who think of Tahiti merely as an isle of luxury, where everything seems to have been created for sensual pleasure and the gratification of the appetites—those, I say, know nothing of the real charm of that land.

Nor those, again—and the greater number, no doubt—who look on Tahiti from a more worthy or artistic point of view, seeing it as a land of eternal spring, always smiling and poetical, a realm of flowers and fair women—even those comprehend it not. The true charm lies elsewhere; it is not open to all.

Go far away from Papeete, whither civilization has not penetrated; where, under the slender coco-palms, the native Tahitian villages are strown, huts thatched with pandanus-leaves, on the very edge of the coral reef and the immense and solitary ocean. See the tranquil, dreaming hamlets, the groups of natives lounging at the feet of the great trees—silent, passive, and idle, feeding, as it would seem, on the cud of speechless contemplation. Listen to the utter calm of nature, the monotonous, eternal murmur of the breakers on the barrier reef; look at the stupendous scenery, the tors of basalt, the dark forests clinging to the mountain's flank—and all this lost in the midst of a vast, immeasurable solitude—the Pacific.

.   .   .   .

XXI

The first time that Rarahu came to mingle with the damsels of Papeete was one evening of high festival. The queen was giving a grand ball to the officers of a frigate which happened to have put into port.

In the ball-room, open on all sides, the Europeans had already taken their places with the ladies of the court, and the colonial residents, all in their very best.

Outside, in the gardens, there was a great tumult and confusion. All the waiting-women and young girls in holiday dresses, were getting up an upa-upa on a great scale. They meant to dance till daybreak to the sound of the tom-tom, and barefoot, while in the queen's ball-room we were to dance to the strains of a piano, in satin shoes.

And the officers, who had already made friends both within and without, went to and fro, from these to those, without any disguise, and with the strange free-and-easyness which Tahitian manners allow.

Curiosity and, yet more, jealousy had prompted Rarahu to this escapade, long premeditated. Jealousy, a rare passion in Oceania, had stolen deep into her little savage soul. When she fell asleep alone in the heart of her native groves, lying down to rest at sunset under the roof of her old foster-parents, she would wonder what could be going on all the long evening at Papeete, where her friend Loti was passing the hours with Faïmana or Téria, the queen's ladies.—And then there was that princess Ariitéa, in whom her woman's instinct suspected a rival.

" Ia ora na, Loti ! " (all hail, Loti) said a familiar little voice suddenly at my elbow, a voice so young and innocent to be mingling in the turmoil of such a festival. And, greatly surprised, I replied: " Ia ora na, Rarahu ! "

Yes it was she indeed, little Rarahu in her white skirt, holding Tiahoui by the hand. There they were both of them, somewhat alarmed, as it seemed, at finding themselves in so unwonted an assembly, where so many young women turned to look at them. They came up to me with a little mincing air, half-smiling, half-prim—it was easy to see that there was a storm in the air.

" Will you not come to walk with us, Loti? Don't you know us here? And are we not as pretty and as nicely dressed as the others are? "

They knew full well that they were much prettier on the contrary; nay, but for that conviction they would probably never have ventured so far.

" Let us go closer," said Rarahu, " I want to see what the women are doing in the queen's house."

So we three, hand in hand, made our way among muslin tunics and garlands of flowers close to the wide-open windows, to look on a spectacle strange indeed in many ways—a reception at the court of Queen Pomaré.

" Loti," asked Tiahoui, " those—there—what are they doing? " and she pointed to a group of women of paler hue, dressed in long and gaudy robes, who were seated with a number of officers round a table covered with a green cloth; they were handling gold pieces, and squares of pictured card which they slipped lightly between their fingers, while their black eyes never lost their imperturbable expression of insinuating and exotic apathy. Tiahoui knew absolutely nothing of the mysteries of poker and baccarat, nor did she fully master such explanations as I was able to give her.

When the first notes of the piano began to sound in the hot vibrating air, silence fell, and Rarahu listened in an ecstasy. Nothing in the least like this had ever fallen on her ear; her strange eyes dilated with rapture and delight. The tom-tom, too, was silenced, and behind us the crowd gathered noise-lessly; not a sound was to be heard but the rustle of soft dresses, the whirr of the huge moths which fluttered their wings in the flame of the candles, and the far-away roll of the Pacific.

Then in came Ariitéa leaning on the arm of an English captain and ready to waltz.

"She is very handsome," said Rarahu in a whisper.

"Very handsome, Rarahu," said I.

"And you are going to this ball, and it will be your turn presently to dance with her and hold her in your arms, while Rarahu must go home alone with Tiahoui, to sleep at Apiré!

"No! Loti, I say you shall not!" she exclaimed with a burst of sudden excitement. "I came to fetch you away!"

"But you will see, Rarahu, how well the piano sounds when I play on it; you will hear me make music, and you never have heard any so sweet. Then you must go because it is growing late. To-morrow will soon come, and to-morrow we shall meet again...."

" By Heaven, Loti, you shall not go ! " she repeated, and her childish voice trembled with fury.

Then, with the swift petulance of a vicious indignant kitten, she snatched off my gold lace, crumpled my collar, and tore down the spotless front of my British shirt.

In short, in this plight I obviously could not present myself at the queen's ball; I had no choice but to put a good face on ill-fortune and go with Rarahu, laughing as I went, away to the groves of Apiré.

But when we were alone in the country far from the sounds of the revel, in the wild wood and the darkness, all about me struck me as absurd and dull —the calm night, the sky bright with unfamiliar stars, the perfume of the island vegetation—everything, even the tones of the lovely little creature at my side. I was dreaming of Ariitéa in her long blue satin tunic, waltzing at the queen's ball, and I longed vehemently to be with her. Rarahu had made a mistake in dragging me away that evening to her woodland solitude.

XXII

LOTI TO HIS SISTER AT BRIGHTBURY

" Dear little Sister : I, too, am under the spell— the wonderful charm of this country, so unlike every other. I fancy I see it now as George used to see it, through the same transfiguring prism. It is hardly two months since I first set foot on the island, and already I am bewitched. The disappointment of the first few days is now a thing of the past, and this, I believe is the spot of earth where, like Mignon, I fain would live to love—and die.

"We have still six months to stay here; the admiral decided that yesterday, and he, like the rest of us, is glad to find himself here rather than elsewhere. The *Reindeer* is not to sail before October; between this and then I shall have grown so used to this gently enervating life that I shall be more than half a native, and I fear it will be a dreadful wrench when at last we must depart.

"I cannot begin to tell you of all the strange impressions I feel as, at every step, I recognize things I remember from the time when I was twelve years old. As a small boy at home I was always dreaming of the South Seas; through the fantastic shroud of the unknown I guessed it, felt it, just what to-day I find it.

"I had seen it all; I knew all their names; the people I meet are those who haunted my childish visions; nay, sometimes I fancy that this is the dream.

"Look through George's papers for a faded photograph of a little cabin on the seashore, built at the foot of some gigantic coco-palms, and half-buried in the greenwood.—It was his. It still stands as you see it. It was pointed out to me, but that was unnecessary. I should have recognized it at once.

"Since he left, it has remained empty; the sea-breezes and the lapse of years have racked and shaken it; the brushwood has smothered it, vanilla creepers shroud it, but it is still known by George's Tahitian name : ' Rouéri's cabin,' it is called to this day. And Rouéri's name is held in honour by many of the natives, more particularly by the queen, who loves me and makes much of me for his memory's sake. You, my dear, were in George's confidence; you knew no doubt that a Tahitian woman whom he loved lived with him during his four years of exile.

" I, who was then but a child, had a guess though I was told nothing. Indeed, I knew that she wrote to him, for I had seen letters lying on his writing-table, in an unknown tongue, which, however, I am now beginning to speak and to understand.

" Her name was Taïmaha. She lives not far off, in a neighbouring island, and I should like to see her. I have often wished to recover trace of her—and now, at the last moment, I hesitate. An indefinable feeling, a sort of scruple checks me at the moment when I am about to stir the ashes and enquire into the past privacy of my brother's life, over which Death has cast a sanctifying shroud.   .   .   ."

XXIII

SOCIAL ECONOMY AND PHILOSOPHY

The temper of the Tahitians is a good deal like that of children; they are whimsical, perverse, suddenly sulky for no reason at all, always honest and well-meaning, and hospitable in the widest scope of the word.

The contemplative side of man is strangely developed in them; they are alive to every aspect of nature, sad or gay, and open to all the vagaries of imagination. The solitude of the woods and darkness terrify them; they people the wilderness with ghosts and spirits.

Night-bathing is a custom in high esteem in Tahiti; parties of young girls go out into the woods by moonlight to plunge into the natural pools of deliciously cold water. And at such an hour a single word: " Toupapahou! " spoken in the midst of the bathers, sends them all flying like crazy creatures. Toupapahou is the name of one of the tattooed bogeys which are the terror of all Polynesians—an uncanny name, terrifying and untranslatable.

In Oceania toil is a thing unknown. The forests spontaneously produce all that is needed for the support of these unforeseeing races; the fruit of the bread-tree, and wild bananas grow for all the world to pluck, and suffice for their need. The years glide over the Tahitians in utter idleness and perpetual dreaming, and these grown-up children could never conceive that in our grand Europe there should be so many people wearing out their lives in earning their daily bread.

XXIV

A CLOUD

The heedless, idle party were all together by the Apiré brook, and Tétouara, who was in her most farcical vein, was pouring forth a flood of Rabelaisian jests at us all, as we lay, half-asleep, in the long grass—stuffing herself all the while with coconuts and oranges. Nothing could be heard but her cackling tones, mingling with the chirrup of the grasshoppers chanting their midday song, at the very hour when, on the opposite side of this earthly globe, my old friends were coming out of the Paris theatres, chilled and muffled, into the icy fog of a winter's night.

Nature was calm and languid; a warm breeze softly swept over the crowns of the trees, and a swarm of little flecks of sunlight danced lightly over us, multiplied to infinity by the broken screen of guava and mimosa-leaves.

Suddenly we saw coming towards us a figure dressed in a flowing tunic of palest green gauze, her long black hair carefully braided, and a wreath of jasmine on her brow. The thin robe betrayed the outlines of a figure never confined by any tighter garment, and under it could also be seen a magnificent *pareo* bound about her hips, the large white flowers on a scarlet ground showing through the light gauze.

I had never seen Rarahu looking so handsome, nor so much in earnest about herself. She was hailed with warm admiration, and in fact she was exceedingly pretty just so, and her shy self-consciousness added to her charm.

She came straight up to me, confused and bashful; then she sat down on the grass by my side and remained quite still, a flush tinging her brown cheeks, her eyes cast down, like a naughty child frightened lest she should be questioned and put to shame.

"Loti, you do things in style!" said one and another of the spectators. And the young women, who had noticed my surprise, were smothering little fits of laughter and giggling among the long grass in a way which implied no end of spiteful suggestions. Tétouara, sharp and pitiless, pronounced judgment on the fine gauze dress in these astute words: "It is made of Chinese stuff!"

And the laughter waxed louder; it came out from behind the guava-bushes, it came up from the waters of the brook;—it was heard on all sides—and poor little Rarahu was very near crying.

XXV

STILL A CLOUD

"It is made of Chinese stuff!" Tétouara had said.

Terrible words, full of hidden meaning, keen-edged words, with a triple barb, which I could not help thinking of again and again.

In point of fact this green gauze dress was quite

new to me; and Rarahu's old adoptive parents, who lived half-naked in a hovel thatched with pandanus, were not likely to have rushed into such lavish splendour.

So I lay lost in thought.

Now, the Chinese merchants of Papeete are an object of disgust and horror to the Tahitian women; there is no greater disgrace for any girl than to be found out in listening to the addresses of one of these men. But they are sly, and they are rich, and it is a well-known fact that by dint of gifts and silver coin many of them win favours which amply compensate them for the scorn of the public.

However, I took good care not to hint this horrible suspicion to John, who would have heaped anathemas on the head of my little Rarahu. I had tact enough neither to reproach her nor to cause a scandal, reserving the right to wait and watch.

XXVI

THE CLOUD DARKENS

One day when I came to the Apiré fall, to our own particular bathing-place under the guava-trees, it was half-past three, not the usual hour. I had come to the spot noiselessly. I pushed aside the branches and looked.—Amazement rooted me to the spot.

There was a horrible thing there, in this place

which we thought of as belonging to ourselves alone;
an old Chinaman, quite naked, was washing his ugly
yellow body in the clear waters of our bath.

He seemed quite at home and did not disturb himself. He had twisted up his long pig-tail of iron-grey
hair and had knotted it, like a woman's, on the very
top of his bald skull. And there, in our stream, he
was washing his bony limbs, which looked as if they
were stained with saffron,—and the sun shone on
him just the same, shedding a softened green light,
—and the clear, cool water whispered round him
just the same,—as naturally and as merrily as if
it were for us.

XXVII

I, posted behind the brushwood, stood watching.
Curiosity kept me there, attentive and motionless.
I had condemned myself to witness the performance,
anxiously wondering what was to come of it.

I had not to wait long. A light rustle of boughs,
a chirping of voices, soon announced the approach
of the two little girls.

The Chinaman, who also heard them, sprang up
as if moved by a spring. Whether from a sense of
decency, or from shame at displaying so much ugliness to the light of the sun, he ran to get his clothes;
the endless muslin garments, worn one over the
other, which composed his costume, were hanging
here and there on the boughs of the trees. He had
time to slip on two or three by the time the girls
came.

Rarahu's cat, leading the procession, humped its back in a very significant fashion when it caught sight of the yellow man, and turned tail in high dudgeon.

Next came Tiahoui; she paused for a moment, putting her hand to her chin and laughing in her sleeve, as having seen something very funny.

Rarahu looked over her shoulder and laughed too. And then they both boldly came forward, saying in saucy tones :

" Ia ora na, Tsin Lee!—Ia ora na tinito, mafatu meiti."*

They knew him by name, and he had called her Rarahu!—He let his long grey pig-tail down with a most coquettish air, and his sensual old eyes glittered with an odious leer.

XXVIII

Out of his pockets he pulled a quantity of things which he offered the little maids;—little boxes of pink or white powder, complicated little instruments for the toilet, little silver scrapers for cleaning the tongue, and he explained their uses,—and then Chinese sugar-plums—fruits preserved with peppers and ginger.

Rarahu especially was the object of his ardent attentions, and the two girls, though they needed some coaxing, accepted the things with no end of little scornful airs, turning up their noses like marmosets.

* Good-day, Tsin Lee, good-day, Chinaman, my sweetheart.

There was a broad pink ribband for which Rarahu suffered him to kiss her bare shoulder.—And then Tsin Lee wanted to go further and put his lips close to my little friend's—but she fled at top speed, followed by Tiahoui. They vanished among the shrubs like a pair of gazelles, their hands full of gifts; I could hear them giggling through the greenery; and Tsin Lee, who could not follow them, remained where he was, chapfallen and out of countenance.

XXIX

THE CLOUD BURSTS

Next day Rarahu, with her head on my knees, wept hot tears. All notion of right and wrong was very imperfect in her little heart; she had grown up at haphazard in the woods; her ideas were confused, outlandish, and unformed, sprouting as they could in the shade of the great trees. Still, they were for the most part sweet and pure, and among them were some Christian notions picked up here and there in her old granny's Bible. Vanity and greediness had led her astray from the right path, but I was sure, perfectly sure, that she had made no return for these ill-omened gifts and all the evil could be washed out by tears. She quite understood that what she had done was very naughty, and above all she understood that she had grieved me—and that John, my solemn brother John, would not look at her with his blue eyes.

She confessed everything, the story of the green

gauze gown, and the red *pareo*. She cried, poor little thing, cried with all her heart; her bosom heaved with sobs, and Tiahoui cried too at the sight.

These tears, the first Rarahu had ever shed, produced the very common result of tears—they made us love each other more than ever. My heart had a larger share in my feelings towards her, and for a while the image of Ariitéa became dim.

This strange little being weeping at my knee, in the solitude of a Polynesian forest, assumed a new aspect in my eyes; for the first time I thought of her as *somebody,* and I began to perceive what an adorable creature she might have become if she had been in other hands than those of two old savages.

XXX

From that day Rarahu, no longer regarding herself a child, ceased to run about with her bosom bare to the sun; even on days which were not holidays she would wear a gown and plait her long hair.

XXXI

Mata-reva was the name Rarahu had given me, not choosing to call me by that of Loti, bestowed by Faïmana or Ariitéa. Mata being exactly interpreted, means an eye; it is by their eyes that this

race designates people, and the names they hit upon
are often very happy. Thus Plunket was called,
Mata-pifaré (cat's eye); Brown was Mata-ioré
(rat's eye), and John Mata-ninamu (blue eye).
Rarahu would not have me called after any animal;
the poetical name of Mata-reva was her choice after
much hesitation. I consulted the dictionary of the
worthy brothers Picpus, and I found this:

Reva, firmament; abyss, depth; mystery.

XXXII

LOTI'S DIARY

The hours, days, months, flew in this land as they
do nowhere else; time slipped on without leaving any
trace, in the monotony of perpetual summer. It
was as though I were in an atmosphere of unchang-
ing calm, where the turmoil of the world had ceased
to exist.

Oh! those delicious hours—the summer hours,
sweet and warm, which we spent, day after day, by
the Fataoua brook, in that nook in the woods, so
shady and out of ken, which was the nest of Rarahu
and Tiahoui. The stream rippled softly over the
polished pebbles, carrying down whole colonies of
microscopic fish and water-flies. The earth was
carpeted with fine grasses, little delicate herbs which
gave out a scent like that of hay in Europe in the
sweet month of June; a delicious fragrance for
which in Tahitian there is a word " poumiriraïra,"

meaning a sweet smell of grass. The air was loaded
with tropical perfume, that of oranges predominat-
ing, oranges heated as they hung on the bough by
the southern sun.

Nothing disturbed the silence of this Oceanian
noon. Little lizards, as blue as turquoises, made
bold by our stillness, shot in and out close by us,
and black butterflies with large violet eyes on their
wings. Not a sound was to be heard but the dimp-
ling fall of water, the subdued twitter of birds, and
from time to time, the dropping of an overripe
guava-fruit, which smashed on the ground with a
scent of raspberries.

And as the day went on, when the sinking sun
cast a more golden glow on the boughs, Rarahu and
I would go home to the solitary hut in the wood.
The two old folks, her foster-parents, stolid and
grave, were always to be seen there, squatting in
front of the pandanus thatch and watching us
arrive. A sort of mystical smile, an expression of
indifferent benevolence would light up their dulled
faces for a moment.

"We greet thee, Loti!" they would say in a
guttural voice; or "We greet thee, Mata-reva!"

And that was all. I had to go, leaving my little
friend with them, while she gazed upon me with
smiling eyes, and looked the very incarnation of
fresh youth by the side of those two gloomy Polynesian mummies.

Then it was supper-time. Old Tahaapaïru would
stretch out his long tattooed arms towards a pile
of dead wood; he would take two pieces of dry

bourao and rub them together to make fire—an old savage way of doing it. Rarahu took the burning wood from the old man's hands, lighted a bundle of small wood and cooked a couple of bread-fruits in an oven in the ground; this was the family meal.

By this time the party of bathers from the Fataoua river were going home to Papeete, Tétouara at their head, and I always had plenty of gay company on my way back.

"Loti," said Tétouara, " do not forget that you are expected this evening in the queen's gardens. Téria and Faïmana told me to say that they count on you to take them to have tea at the Chinese tea-house—and I will go with pleasure, if you please."

So we went home singing, along a road whence we looked out on the wide blue ocean, lighted by the last gleams of the setting sun. Night fell on Tahiti, translucent and star-lit. Rarahu was asleep in the wood; the crickets set up their evening concert in the grass, moths circled under the great trees—and the queen's women were airing themselves in the palace gardens.

XXXIII

One day when Rarahu was walking with me in one of the shady avenues of the town, she bid good-day in a way half-friendly, half-scornful, and a little frightened too, to an outlandish creature who passed us. It was a tall thin woman, with nothing of the Tahitian about her but the costume; she bowed in return with stiff dignity, and turned round to look at us. Rarahu, much vexed, put out her tongue at her, and then she told me that this old maid, a half-breed, a lanky mixture of English and Maori, had been her teacher at the school at Papeete.

One day the half-caste woman had told her pupil that she had the highest hopes of seeing her succeed to this high office, by reason of the facility with which the child learnt everything. Rarahu, stricken with terror at the idea of such a prospect, suddenly took to her heels and fled to Apiré, quitting the school-house at once, never to return.

XXXIV

One morning I returned on board the *Reindeer*, full of the sensational announcement that I had slept in the same room with Tamatoa.

Tamatoa, the eldest son of Queen Pomaré—husband of the fair Queen Moé of the island of Raïatéa, and father of the bewitching little invalid Pomaré V.—was a man who for many years had been kept shut up within four strong walls, and who was still a mythical terror in the land. In his normal state, Tamatoa, it was said, was not more wicked than other men; but he drank, and when he was drunk " he saw red "—he must have blood.

He was about thirty years of age, immensely big and a Hercules in strength; several men together could not hold him when he had once lost his head; he cut throats without rhyme or reason, and his atrocities were beyond all imagining.

And yet Pomaré worshipped this colossal son of

hers. It was even whispered that of late she had been known to open the door for him, and that he had been seen prowling about the gardens at night. His presence gave the women about the court the same sort of terror as a wild beast might whose cage was known to be insecure at night.

There was in the palace a strangers' room, open night and day; the floor was strewn with mattresses covered with clean white mats, on which Tahitian visitors would sleep, belated chiefs from the outlying districts, and I myself occasionally.

All was silent in the palace and grounds when I went into the strangers' shelter. I found there but one other person, a man seated with his elbows on a table on which burnt a coco-nut-oil lamp. He was a stranger of supernatural height and build; with one hand he could have crushed a man like glass. He had huge square cannibal jaws; his big head was savage and grim, his eyes, half shut, had a look of wandering melancholy.

"Ia ora na, Loti," said the man. I stopped in the doorway. Then began the following dialogue, in Tahitian, between the stranger and me:

"How do you know my name?"

"I know that you are Loti, the little fellow who wears gold lace and goes about with the white-haired admiral. I have often seen you go by in the evening.—You have come to sleep here?"

"And you? You are the chief of some island?"

"Yes, I am a great chief.—Lie down in that corner; that is the best mat."

When I had lain down, rolled in my *paréo*, I shut my eyes—just enough to watch this strange individual who had risen cautiously and stolen over to look at me. At the same moment a slight noise made me turn my head the other way, towards the door, where the old queen had just come in; she walked with the utmost caution on the tip of her bare toes, but the mats creaked under the weight of her heavy person.

When the man was close to me he took a mosquito curtain which he carefully spread above my head; then he placed a banana-leaf in front of his lamp to screen the light from my eyes, and went back to his seat, resting his head in his hands again. Pomaré, who had watched us both with evident anxiety, hidden in the dark doorway, seemed satisfied with what she had seen, and disappeared.

The queen never came to this part of the palace, and her appearance having confirmed me in the idea that my companion was not to be trusted cured me of all desire to sleep. The stranger, however, did not stir; his eyes were vague and vacant; he had forgotten my existence. In the distance I could hear some of the queen's women singing a *himéné* of the Pomotous Islands. And presently the big voice of old Ariifaité, the prince-consort, called out, " Mamou! Silence!—It is midnight! " And all was silent as if by magic.

An hour later the figure of the old queen was again visible in the doorway. The lamp was dying out and the man had fallen asleep.

I very soon did the same, though my slumbers were light; and when, at day-break, I rose to go, I saw that he had not moved; only his head had sunk and was resting on the table.

I had a bath in a rivulet of cool water under a clump of acacias at the bottom of the garden, and then went to the verandah to pay my respects to the queen and thank her for her hospitality.

" Haere mai, Loti," said she as soon as she could see me.   " Come here, and let us have a chat."

" Well," she went on, " did he treat you well? "

" Yes," said I, and I saw her old face beam when I expressed my acknowledgments of the care he had taken of me.

" Do you know who it was," she said in a mysterious whisper.   " Oh ! never tell, my little Loti, but it was Tamatoa."

A few days after this Tamatoa was officially declared free—on condition that he should not quit the palace.—I often met him and shook hands with him.

This went on till the day when he evaded the guards and murdered a woman and two children in the garden of the Protestant missionary, and then in the course of one single day committed a series of sanguinary horrors which could not be written down—not even in Latin.

XXXV

Who can tell where the charm of this land resides? Who can lay his finger on the secret and intangible something, for which no human tongue has a name?

. . . .

In the spell of Tahiti there is something of the weird sadness which hangs over all these Oceanian isles,—their isolation in the vast, far-off Pacific,—the sea-wind,—the moan of the breakers,—the density of shade—the hoarse, melancholy voices of the islanders, who wander, singing, among the trunks of the coco-palms which are so amazingly tall, and white, and slender.

In vain do we try to seize—to understand—to express the feeling. It is useless; the secret evades us and is not to be unveiled.

I have written pages, many and long, about Tahiti; in them there are endless details, even as to the appearance of the tiniest plants—the physiognomy of its mosses.

You may read it all with the best will in the world, —well, and then—do you understand? No—not in the least. Has this helped you to hear, at night, on the Polynesian shores white with coral—to hear, at night, the plaintive sound of the *vivo* (the reed pipe) from the very depth of the woods—or the distant bellowing of conch-shell trumpets?

XXXVI

GASTRONOMICAL

" The flesh of white man tastes like ripe bananas." —This information was given me by the old Maori chief Hoatoaru, of Routoumah, whose judgment on the subject is beyond dispute.

XXXVII

Rarahu, in a fit of exasperation had called me *a long lizard without feet,* and just at first I had not quite understood. The serpent being a creature absolutely unknown in Polynesia, the half-breed who had educated Rarahu, to explain to her the form under which the devil had tempted the first woman, had made use of this description. So Rarahu was in the habit of thinking of the long lizard without feet as the most wicked and dangerous of terrestrial creatures, and that was why she had flung the words in my teeth.

She was still jealous, poor little Rarahu; it troubled her to think that Loti could care for any one else. The evenings at Papeete, with their pleasures in which her old guardians would not allow her to mingle, set her childish imagination working. Above all, the tea-drinks in the Chinese tea-houses, of which Tétouara brought her the most exciting descriptions—tea-drinkings where Téria, Faïmana and others of the wild girls who attended the old queen, drank—nay, and were drunk. And Loti would go, would sometimes even preside, and this utterly puzzled Rarahu, till she gave it up.

When she had abused me roundly she cried—a far more effectual argument.

From that day forth I was never to be seen at the evenings at Papeete. I stayed later in the Apiré woods, sometimes sharing the bread-fruit with old Tahaapaïru. Night-fall was melancholy enough in this wilderness, but its sadness had a peculiar charm, and Rarahu's voice sounded delightfully in the evening under the high, gloomy vault of trees. I used to stay till the hour when the old folks said their prayer—a prayer in an uncanny savage brogue, but the same as I had been taught in my childhood: "Our Father which art in Heaven,"—the sublime, eternal prayer of the Lord rang out in a strangely mysterious manner out there, at the antipodes of the old world, in the darkness of that forest, the silence of those nights, spoken in the strong bass tones of this bogey old man.

XXXVIII

There was one thing which Rarahu was already beginning to feel, and which she was fated to feel bitterly later; a thing she was incapable of formulating with any precision in her own mind, and yet more of expressing in the terms of her primitive tongue. She apprehended vaguely that there must be gulfs, in the intellectual order, fixed between Loti and herself, whole worlds of undreamed-of ideas and knowledge. She already appreciated the difference of our race, of our notions, of our lightest emotions. On the most elementary details of life our ideas differed widely. Loti, though dressed as a Tahitian and speaking her language, was still to her a *Paoupa*—that is to say, one of the men who come from the impossible lands beyond the ocean, one of the men who, within the last few years, have brought so many undreamed-of changes and unforeseen novelties into the stagnancy of Polynesia.

Then, too, she knew that Loti would soon go away, never to return—go away to his own remote country. She had no conception of those bewildering distances,—and Tahaapaïru compared them to that which divides Fataoua from the moon and the stars.

She never thought of herself as being in Loti's eyes—child of fifteen as she was—anything more than a strange little being, a plaything for a time, soon to be forgotten.

But she was mistaken. Loti was beginning to be aware that he had a feeling for her of a less vulgar stamp. He was beginning to love her, really love her. He remembered his brother George, whom the Tahitians had called Rouéri, who had carried home with him ineradicable memories of this land, and he felt that he should do the same. It seemed to Loti quite possible that this love-affair, set going at a venture by a whim of Tétouara's might leave deep and permanent traces on his whole life.

While yet very young, Loti had been cast on the stormy tide of European life; at a very early age he had lifted the curtain which hides the drama of the world from infant eyes; launched at the age of sixteen on the whirlpool of London and Paris, he had suffered at an age when most lads have scarcely begun to think. Loti had withdrawn from this campaign in the dawn of his life very weary, and believing himself already quite used up. He had been very thoroughly sickened and disappointed because, before this change into a youth like other young men, he had been an innocent and dreamy child, brought up in the pure peace of family life; he, too, had been a little savage, on whose heart in his isolation a multitude of fresh ideas and bright illusions had set their mark. Before going off to dream in the groves of Oceania, he had long dreamed as a child in the Yorkshire woods.

There were numberless mysterious affinities between Loti and Rarahu, born at opposite extremities of the earth. Both had the habit of seclusion and contemplation, both were used to woods and nature's solitudes; both were quite happy spending long hours in silence, reclining on moss and flowers; both were passionately addicted to day-dreams, music, fine fruit, flowers, and running water.

XXXIX

And for the present there was not a cloud on the horizon. We still had five long months before us. It was quite useless to look forward to the future.

XL

It was delightful when Rarahu would sing.

When she sang alone there were in her voice certain notes so fresh and so sweet that only birds or little children have the like. When she sang with others she could execute, above the air sung by the rest, little extravagant variations on the very highest notes of the scale, always very elaborate and admirably true.

At Apiré, as in every district of Tahiti, there was a choir known as the "*himéné*," which performed regularly under the direction of a conductor and was to be heard at all the native festivals. Rarahu was one of the chief performers, and held the first place by her pure voice.—The chorus which sang the accompaniment was deep and husky; the men, especially, put in strange low metallic notes, and a sort of roar, marking the dominants, and resembling the sound of some savage instrument rather than the human voice. But as a whole their precision was enough to infuriate the pupils of the Conservatoire at Paris, and in the woods, after dark, the effect was something quite beyond description.

XLI

Day was declining. I was alone by the sea, on a part of the shore near Apiré. In this deserted spot I was waiting for Taïmaha, and felt mysteriously excited by the thought that this woman was coming.

Taïmaha, I had been told, had come to Tahiti the day before. An old hag who had known her in former years, in Rouéri's hut, had bidden me to meet her here and had undertaken to let her know.

Presently a woman appeared, who, seeing me under the coco-palms, came towards me. It was now dark, but when she was quite close I saw a hideous face looking at me with the odious grin of a savage.

"Are you Taïmaha?" said I.

"Taïmaha? No. My name is Tevaruefaipo-tuaiahutu, and I came from Papetoaï. I have come to gather cowries on the reef, and pink coral. Will you buy some?"

I lingered there till midnight.

Next day I learnt that Taïmaha had gone back to her island at daybreak; my commission remained unfulfilled. She was gone, never dreaming that Rouéri's brother had waited for her for many hours on the sea-shore.

XLII

LOTI TO JOHN B., ON BOARD THE " REINDEER "

TARAVAO, 1872.

"Good brother John : The messenger who delivers this letter has also a heap of presents I am sending you; a tuft of feathers made from the tails of the scarlet phaeton, a very precious curiosity and the gift of my host, the chief of Tehaupoo; then a neck-lace of three rows of little white shells given me by his lady wife; finally, two bunches of *reva-reva*, which a great lady of the district of Papéouriri stuck on my head yesterday at a feast at Taravao.

"I shall stay here a few days longer, with the chief, who was a friend of my brother; and I shall take as long leave as I can get the admiral to give me. I only want you here, my dear fellow, to be perfectly enchanted with my stay at Taravao. The neighbourhood of Papeete can give you no notion of this unknown quarter of the island, the peninsula of Taravao; a peaceful nook, shady and bewitching; groves of enormous orange-trees, their fruit and flowers strewing the earth, which is carpeted with soft grass and pink periwinkle.

"Under the trees a few huts lie scattered, built of lemon-tree wood and inhabited by the immutable aborigines. In these we still find the old indigenous hospitality, meals of fruit laid out under green awnings of plaited boughs and flowers; music too, reed *vivos* in plaintive unison, and a chorus of *himénés,* singing and dancing.

"I live alone in a solitary hut built on piles over the sea and corals. By leaning out of my bed of white matting I can look down into the strange busy world of the reef. Among white and pink branches, and the elaborate tangle of madrepores, myriads of tiny fish flit to and fro, their colours vieing with those of gems or of humming-birds—geranium-scarlet, vivid Chinese green, blues which no paint could reproduce—besides swarms of other creatures of every hue, and of every shape excepting that of a fish. By day, during the hours of siesta, lost in contemplation I can admire all these things which are almost unknown even to naturalists and observers.

"At night I feel a little chill about the heart in this Robinson Crusoe-like solitude. When the wind is whistling outside, when the great complaining of the sea comes up through the darkness, then a sort of anguish of loneliness comes over me out here at the southern-most and most forsaken point of this distant isle, face to face with the immensity of the Pacific—*the* immensity of all earthly immensities, spreading away to the occult shores of the south-polar continent.

" During an excursion of two days, in the society of the chief of Tehaupoo, I saw the lake of Vaïria which fills the natives with superstitious terrors. We encamped for one night on its bank. It is a strange spot which few people have seen; only a few Europeans find their way hither at long intervals out of curiosity; the way is long and toilsome, the approach wild and desolate. Picture to yourself, at a thousand yards above the ocean, a dead sea buried among the mountains in the middle of the island; all round rise high, austere bluffs, their masses standing out in sharp outline against a clear evening sky. The water is clear and deep, nothing is stirring —not even a fish. 'Of old,' said the chief of Tehaupoo, ' Toupapahous of a peculiar race used to come down from the mountains at night and beat the water with great albatross-wings.'

" If you call on the governor on Wednesday evening you will meet Princess Ariitéa. Tell her that I do not forget her in my solitude, and that I hope to dance with her next week at the queen's ball. If you should happen to come across Faïmana or Téria in the gardens you may say whatever comes into your head—on my behalf.

" Now, my dear old fellow, will you do me the kindness of going to the brook of Fataoua, and give me some news of little Rarahu, of Apiré. Do this for me, I beg and pray. You are too kind not to understand, and to forgive us both. Poor little thing ! On my honour I love her with all my heart."

XLIII

Rarahu knew nothing of the god Taaroa nor of the numerous goddesses in his train; she had never even heard of any of the personages of Polynesian mythology. Queen Pomaré alone, out of respect for the traditions of her country, had learnt the names of those old-world deities and preserved in her mind some of the strange legends of the bygone days.

But all those strange words of the Tahitian tongue which had struck me by their vague or mystical import, having no equivalent in our European languages, were household words to Rarahu, who would use them and explain them to me with rare and remarkable poetical feeling.

"If you stayed at Apiré oftener at night," she said to me, "you would learn much more quickly of me, a number of words which the girls who live at Papeete do not know. And when we are frightened together I will teach you the most terrible things about the Toupaphous—things you never heard of!"

In fact there are in the Maori tongue many words and metaphors which only become intelligible by degrees, after living with the islanders at night in the woods, listening to the murmur of the wind and the sea, the ear attent for every mysterious voice of nature.

XLIV

No song of birds is to be heard in the Tahitian forest; this innocent music, which in other latitudes fills the groves with life and gaiety, is unknown to Polynesian ears. Under the dense shade, among the creepers and tree-ferns nothing flies, nothing stirs; all is silent,—a strange silence which seems to sit brooding on the melancholy fancy of the natives. But in the rocky defiles, high, fearfully high overhead, the phaeton is to be seen, a small white bird with a long rose-coloured or white feather in its tail.

Formerly the chiefs used to stick a tuft of these feathers in their head-dresses, and it needed time and patience to acquire this high-caste decoration.

XLV

Rarahu and Tiahoui had been abusing each other roundly. For several minutes their fresh lips had poured forth, without pause or hesitation, a flood of the most childish and most absurd vituperations— the most gross, too, for Tahitian, like Latin, " in words, defies decency."

It was their first quarrel, and it afforded great amusement to the gallery. All the young women stretched on the shore of the brook of Fataoua were in fits of laughing and spurred them on.

"You are a lucky dog, Loti," said Tétouara. " They are quarrelling for you! "

And so in fact they were; Rarahu had had a

sudden fit of jealousy of Tiahoui, and so the dispute had begun.

The two little girls glared at each other like two cats about to spring and roll and scratch; quite pale, rigid but quivering with rage.

"*Tinito oufa!*" (Chinaman's darling!), cried Tiahoui, having exhausted all her arguments, with cruel allusion to the fine green gauze dress.

"*Oviri, Amutaata!*" (savage, cannibal!), retorted Rarahu, who knew that her friend had come as an infant from one of the remotest Pomotous islands, and that though Tiahoui was not a cannibal, certainly some of her kith and kin had been.

The taunt had hit true on either side, and the two little maids, clutching each other by the hair, scratched and bit. They were soon separated; then they began to cry; and finally, Rarahu having thrown herself into Tiahoui's arms, the two little things, who were devoted friends, ended by embracing each other fondly.

XLVI

Tiahoui, in her effusiveness had embraced Rarahu by rubbing noses, after an old Maori fashion now obsolete, which was a reminiscence of her childhood and her barbarous home. She put her little nose against Rarahu's round cheek and sniffed hard. Thus, by sniffing, the South Sea Islanders were wont to embrace; kissing with the lips they learnt from Europeans. And Rarahu, in the midst of her tears gave me a comical glance and a smile of understanding, as much as to say:

" Do you see this little savage! Was I not right, Loti, to call her so?—But I love her dearly all the same." And the two little girls clasped each other fondly, and in a few minutes all was forgotten.

XLVII

Wandering along the white strand of Tahiti, under the slim coco-palms, now and again, on some solitary headland where we look out on the blue immensity, in some spot chosen by the melancholy taste of forgotten generations, we come on funereal knolls, great barrows of coral. These are the *maraé*, the tombs of long departed chiefs; the history of the dead who sleep below is lost in the fabulous and unknown past which preceded the discovery of the islands of Polynesia. These *maraé* are to be met with on the shores of all the islands inhabited by the Maori race.

The mysterious islanders of Rapa-Nui decorated these burial places with gigantic statues wearing horrible masks; the Tahitians only planted groves of iron-trees. The iron-tree is the cypress of those islands; its foliage is dark and melancholy; the sea-wind wails curiously in its stiff boughs. These mounds, perfectly white in spite of the lapse of ages, the dead white of coral, and crowned by tall black trees, record the memory of the terrible religion of the past, for they also served as altars on which human victims were slain in honour of the dead.

" Tahiti," Pomaré told me, " was the only island where, even in the earliest times, the victims were not eaten after they were slaughtered; only a semblance of the gruesome feast was held, and the eyes, removed from their sockets, were placed together on a dish and served to the queen,"—a hideous prerogative of sovereignty. (This I heard from Pomaré herself.)

XLVIII

Tahaapaïru, Rarahu's adoptive father, carried on such a strange trade that in our Europe, fertile as it is in every kind of invention, nothing of the kind was ever heard or thought of.

He was very old, which is not very common in Oceania, and he had moreover a beard, and that a white one, a great rarity in those parts. In the Marquesas a white beard is an almost undiscoverable rarity, used in the manufacture of certain precious adornments for the head and ears of some of the chiefs, and old men are carefully maintained and taken care of for the sake of the produce of their chins, which is cut at regular intervals. Twice a year old Tahaapaïru cut off his beard and exported it to Hivaoa, the most savage of the Marquesas isles, where he sold it for its weight in gold.

XLIX

Rarahu was gazing with interest and terror at a skull which lay on my knees. We were sitting on the very top of a coral tumulus at the foot of the huge iron-trees. It was evening, in the remote district of Papenoo; the sun was slowly dipping towards the vast green ocean, in the midst of the great silence of nature.

I looked at Rarahu with unwonted tenderness that evening. The next day I was going away for some time; the *Reindeer* was to make a cruise to the north of the Marquesas archipelago.

Rarahu, wordless and dreamy, was lost in one of those childlike fits of brooding which I never wholly succeeded in understanding. For a moment her whole figure was lighted up with a golden glory; in the next the sun was swallowed up by the ocean, and her figure stood forth a slender, graceful silhouette against the western sky.

Rarahu had never before looked so closely at the lugubrious object which lay in my lap, and which to her, as to every Polynesian, was a thing of horror. It was easy to see that this sinister object roused a crowd of fresh ideas in her mind, though she could not give them any definite form.

The skull must have been very ancient; it was almost a fossil, and tinged with the red hue which the soil of these islands gives to bones. Death has ceased to be loathsome when it is so long ago.

"*Riaria!*" cried Rarahu. A Tahitian word very imperfectly rendered by *awesome,* because it implies the peculiarly gloomy dread which is caused by spectres, or the dead.

"What is there to terrify you so much in this poor skull?" said I to Rarahu.

And she pointed to the toothless jaw and said: "Its laugh, Loti; its laugh—like that of a Tou-papahou."

It was very late at night when we made our way

back to Apiré, and Rarahu had a series of frights all the way home.   In this country where there is absolutely nothing to be afraid of, neither plants, beasts nor men—where, go where you will, you may sleep in the open air, alone and unarmed—the natives are terrified of the night and quake at phantoms.

In the open places and along the strand it was not so bad; Rarahu held my hand tightly in hers and sang *himénés* to keep her courage up.

But there was a certain great grove of coco-palms which was a place of terror.   Rarahu walked in front, making me hold her hands behind her back, not a very convenient arrangement for getting on fast; she felt herself better protected so, and more secure from being seized by the hair by the brick-red death's-head.

It was absolutely dark under the trees, and the wild plants of the wood gave out a sweet smell.   The ground was strewn with dried palm-leaves which crackled under our feet.   Overhead the air was full of a sound peculiar to coco-groves, a metallic rustle of stirring leaves; behind the trees we heard the laughter of the Toupapahous and at our feet a fearsome and startling scurry—the hasty flight of swarms of blue crabs hurrying away at our approach, into their hiding-places underground.

L

Next day was one of exciting leave-takings.

In the evening I expected at last to see Taïmaha;

THE REEF.

Norman H. Hardy.

she had come back to Tahiti, I was told, and I had made an appointment with her through one of the queen's women, to meet on the shore at Fareute at nightfall. When, at the hour fixed, I reached the lonely spot I saw a woman standing motionless and expectant, her face hidden in a thick white veil. I went up to her and called her Taïmaha. The veiled woman let me repeat the name several times without replying; she turned her head away and was laughing under the folds of her muslin wrap.

I pulled the veil away and found the familiar face of Faïmana, who ran off shouting with glee.

Faïmana never told me what assignation had brought her to this spot, where she was ill-pleased to meet me; she had never heard of Taïmaha and could tell me nothing about her. So I had no choice but to postpone any further attempt to see her till my next visit. It seemed as though this woman were a myth, or that some mysterious power took pleasure in keeping us apart, having some more startling meeting in store for a future day.

We weighed anchor next morning a little before daybreak; Tiahoui and Rarahu accompanied me to the shore as the stars began to wane. Rarahu shed floods of tears though the cruise of the *Reindeer* was to last only a month; she, perhaps, had a presentiment that the blissful time we had just passed together could never be repeated.

The idyl was ended. Against all human anticipation those hours of peace and delight we had spent on the shore of the brook of Fataoua were gone, never to return.

PART II

I

NUKA-HIVA; A HORS-D'ŒUVRE

(which the reader may skip, but which is not very long.)

THE mere name of Nuka-Hiva brings with it the notion of a penitentiary and transportation, though at the present day there is nothing to justify this unpleasant association.   Convicts have for many years ceased to inhabit this lovely spot, and the now useless fort of Taïohaé is already in ruins.   This island, which till 1842 was free and savage, since then has belonged to France; dragged down in the fall of Tahiti, of the Society Islands and the Pomotous, it ceased to be independent when those archipelagos surrendered of their own free will.

Taïohaé, the capital, contains perhaps a dozen of Europeans, the governor, the pilot, the missionary bishop, a few friars, four sisters who keep a school for little girls, and finally, four *gendarmes*.

Living in their midst the deposed queen, bereft of her authority, enjoys a pension of six hundred francs a year, with rations for a guard of soldiers for herself and her family.

The South Sea whalers used formerly to choose Taïohaé as a playground, and the place was a prey to their license; rough sailors, set at large, made

75

their way into the huts of the natives and made havoc there. Now, thanks to the imposing presence of the four *gendarmes,* they prefer to descend on other islands.

Nuka-Hiva was at one time populous, but recent importations of European epidemics have more than decimated the islanders. The beauty of their physique is famous, and the natives of the Marquesas are regarded as one of the finest races in the world. However, it takes some little time to accustom the European to their strange faces and to discern their charm. The women, whose figures are so graceful and perfect, have hard features, hewn out, as it were, with a hatchet; and their style of beauty conforms to no recognized standard.

At Taïohaé they wear the long muslin tunic adopted by the Tahitians; their hair is not allowed to grow very long, but stands out in a crisp frizzle; they scent themselves with sandalwood oil. But in the interior this attire is reduced to the last degree of simplicity.

The men wear nothing but a narrow loin-cloth, tattooing being in their eyes an all-sufficient toilet. And certainly they are tattooed with amazing care and art; but a singular freak leads them to confine the elaborate design to one-half of the body, the right or the left, while the other half is left white— or very nearly white. Bands of dark blue outlined on the face give them a grand savage air, contrasting strangely with the white of the eyes and the brilliant sheen of the teeth.

In the neighbouring islands, where Europeans are seldom seen, the wonderful old-world feather head-dresses are still in use, with necklaces of teeth threaded in long rows, and tufts of black wool for ear-rings.

Taïohaé stands at the head of a deep bay, sheltered by tall cliffs and hills of strangely-contorted forms. The densest greenery lies like a splendid mantle over all the land. Throughout the island we find the same close growth of trees and useful or rare timber, while myriads of coco-palms wave their heads high above the forest, perched on their tall slender columns.

The huts—not very many—which constitute the capital are scattered along the shady avenue which follows the indentations of the shore. Behind this lovely road, the only one, a few paths through the wood lead up the hillside. The interior of the island is such a tangle of forest and rock that no one ever goes to see what is going on there, and the only communications are by sea from one bay to another, in the native canoes. But up among the hills perch the old Maori cemeteries, objects of terror to every islander, and the abiding-place of the dreadful Toupapahous.

Few are the passers-by in the high street of Taïohaé; the ceaseless excitement of European life is unknown at Nuka-Hiva. The natives spend chief part of the day squatting outside their cabin doors, as motionless as sphinxes. Like the Tahitians they live on the produce of the forest, and labour is use-less. Some, indeed, from time to time go fishing out of sheer greediness, but most of them would rather not take the trouble.

Popoï, one of their most elaborate dishes, is a barbarous mixture of fruit, fish and crabs, buried in the earth till it begins to ferment. The odour of this concoction is beyond words.

Cannibalism, which still prevails in the neighbouring island of Hivaoa (or Dominica), has for some years ceased in Nuka-Hiva. This happy mitigation of the national customs is due to the efforts of the missionaries; in every other respect the superficial Christianity of the natives has not had the slightest effect on their mode of life, and their debauchery and immorality defy imagination.

Idols of their god are still constantly found in the hands of these islanders, a hideous embryonic shape. The queen has four such images carved on the sticks of her fan.

II

RARAHU'S FIRST LETTER TO LOTI

(Brought to the Marquesas by a whaling ship.)

Apiré i te 10 no mati 1872 Apiré, May 10th 1872.

E Loti, tau taio rahi e, O Loti, my great friend,
E ta u tane iti here rahi, O my dear little husband
ia ora na oe I greet you,
i te Atau mau. by the true God.
  Tau mafatu merahi My heart is very sad
peapea no te mea ua because you are gone so
rave atu oe, far away,
  no te mea aita nau because I see you no
mirimiri faahou ia oe. more.
I tui nei ra, Now I beg you,

O tau hoa iti here rahi,
my dear little friend,

ia tae mau atu teie nei rata ia oe,
when this letter reaches you

e papai noa mai oe ia ù,
to write to me,

ì to oe na mau manao rii,
to make me know your thoughts

ìa mauruuru noa e a vau,
that I may be happy.

E riro ra paha
It has happened perhaps

ua ruri e to oe na manao
that your thoughts have turned from me,

te huru iho a rahoi ìa te taata nei,
as it happens to men here

ìa taa e atu i taua ra vahine.
when they have left their wives.

Aita roa tu e parau rii api
There is nothing new

i Apiré nei,
in Apiré for the present

maori ra e o Turiri,
unless it be that Turiri,

tau pifare iti here rahi,
my dearest little cat,

ua merahi mauiui
is very ill,

epohe paha roa ino ìa oe e haere mai faahou
and will perhaps be quite dead when you come back

Tirara tau parau iti
I have finished my little story.

Ia ora na oe.
I greet you

    Rarahu.
    Rarahu.

III

QUEEN VAEKEHU

Going along the street of Taïohaé to the left, we come to the queen's palace, close to a limpid stream. A banyan fig-tree of enormous extent covers the royal hut with its gloomy shade. Among the gnarled and knotted roots, twisted like writhing reptiles, we discover women seated there, draped in tunics, usually golden-yellow, which gives their skin a coppery hue. Their features are hard and savage; they look up as you approach with an expression of wild irony. There they sit all day, half-asleep, motionless and silent as idols.

This is the court of Nuka-Hiva, Queen Vaékéhu and her ladies.

Under an unattractive exterior these women are gentle and hospitable; they are delighted if a stranger sits down by them, and offer him coco-nuts and oranges.

Elizabeth and Atéria, two who speak French, then ask absurd questions, on behalf of the queen, as to the late war with Germany. They talk loud but slowly, accentuating each word in a way of their own. Battles in which more than a thousand men have fought make them smile incredulously; the size of our armies is beyond their imagining.

The conversation soon languishes; a few phrases are all they care to exchange; their curiosity once satisfied the interview is at an end. The whole court turn to mummies once more, and do what you will to attract attention they pay no further heed.

The royal residence, built by the French government, stands in a lonely clearing in the midst of coco-palms and tamarisk-trees. But close to this modest dwelling, a large native building on the seashore, the ceremonial residence, shows what was the elegance of primitive architecture. On a raised platform of black flagstones huge pillars of magnificent timber support the beams. The walls and roof are formed of boughs of lemon-tree, chosen from among thousands, as straight and polished as reeds, and all the wood is tied together with cords of various colours plaited and twined so as to form complicated and regular patterns. Here again the queen and her waiting-women spend long hours in motionless repose, while they watch their nets drying in the burning sun.

The thoughts which pucker the queen's strange features are a mystery to all; the secret of her endless dreams is impenetrable. Is it melancholy or brutish dulness? Is she really thinking of anything, or not thinking at all? Does she regret her independence and the savage good old time, and the degeneracy and defection of her people? Atéria, who is her shadow, her dog, might perhaps be able to tell, and perhaps this ubiquitous damsel might choose to inform us, but it is more probable that she does not know; nay, she may never have troubled her head about it.

Vaékéhu consented very graciously to sit for her portrait several times, and so placid a sitter never submitted to be studied at leisure.

This fallen queen, with her mane of wavy hair and her haughty reserve, was still a rather grand figure.

IV

DEATH OF VAEKEHU

One evening, as I was making my way by moon-light along one of the paths leading up the hill, the waiting-women hailed me. Their queen, who had long been ill, was going to die they said. She had received extreme unction from the missionary bishop.

Vaékéhu, lying on the ground, was wringing her tattooed arms in great agony; her women, squatting round her with their large towzled heads, were wailing and groaning and making a mourning, to use the expression of the Bible, which perfectly describes their peculiar mode of lamentation.

We rarely see so striking a scene in our cilivized lands. In this bare hut, devoid of all the dismal paraphernalia which in Europe add a terror to death, this woman's end was full of weird poetry and the bitterness of woe.

Very early next morning I left Nuka-Hiva, never to return, not knowing whether its sovereign had gone to join the old tattooed kings her ancestors.

Vaékéhu was the last queen of Nuka-Hiva. Formerly a heathen, and even a cannibal, she had been converted to Christianity and the approach of death had no terrors for her.

V

FUNEREAL

Our absence had lasted just a month—the month of May, 1872. It was quite dark when the *Reindeer* returned to her moorings in the roads of Papeete, on the 1st of June, at eight o'clock in the evening. When, soon after, I set foot on the delightful island, a young woman who seemed to be waiting for me under the deep shade of the bouraos, came forward and said : " Loti, is it you? Do not be uneasy about Rarahu. She is waiting for you at Apiré, where she bid me conduct you. Her mother Huamahine died last week; her father Tahaapaïru died this morning, and she stayed by him with the other women of Apiré to watch the body.

"We have been expecting you every day," Tiahoui went on, " and have often fixed our eyes on the horizon. This evening, at sunset, as soon as we saw the white sails in the offing we knew it was the *Reindeer*. Then we saw it pass Tanoa, and I came down to the shore to wait for you."

We set out by the shore to reach the open country. We walked fast, along paths soaked with rain. It had poured all day—one of the last heavy torrents of the winter season, and masses of black cloud were still riding on the breeze.

On our way Tiahoui informed me that she had been married a fortnight since to a young Tahitian, named Téharo; she had left Apiré to live with her husband at Papéuriri, two days march further to the south-west. Tiahoui was no longer the merry little minx I had known. She talked gravely, and was more of a woman, and more sober.

We soon turned into the woods. The brook of Fataoua, swollen by the rains, growled under the boulders, the wind rocked the dripping boughs overhead and covered us with heavy drops. A light, twinkling from afar among the trees, showed us the hut where lay the corpse of Tahaapaïru.

This cabin, the home of my little friend's childhood, was oval, low, like all the Tahitian huts, and built on a raised floor of black flagstones. The walls were made of slender branches of bourao set upright with intervals between like the bars of a cage. Between them human figures could be seen, all motionless, while the lamp flickering in the wind made their shadows writhe and dance.

Just as I was about to cross the threshold of death Tiahoui pushed me hastily to the right;—I had not seen the long feet of the dead man which lay over it, to the left. I had almost kicked them; I shivered from head to foot and turned away my head to avoid seeing them.

There were five or six women within, seated in a row close to the wall, and in the middle Rarahu keeping an anxious and gloomy eye on the door.

She recognized the sound of my footstep and flew to meet me and drag me out again.

VI

She forgot to be afraid, and we talked in low tones, conscious of the nearness of the dead. We clasped each other in a long and close embrace, and then we sat down on the damp moss, near the hut where the corpse was sleeping.

Rarahu was alone in the world and very forlorn. She had made up her mind to quit the pandanus roof under which the old folks had died—at once—to-morrow.

"Loti," said she, so low that her soft voice was only a whisper in my ear, "Loti, would not you like that we should live together in a house in Papeete? As your brother Rouéri did with Taïmaha, and a great many others too, who are very happy, and with whom neither the governor nor the queen ever find fault. I have no one left in the world but you, and you cannot desert me.—Why, you know there have been men here from your country who liked this life so well that they became Tahitians and never went away. ..."

Yes, I knew that very well; I was well aware of the omnipotent charm of this indolent race, and for that very reason I was rather afraid of it.

Meanwhile the women who had been keeping watch, one by one had stolen noiselessly away, down the forest path. It was growing very late.

"Come in now," said she.

Those long feet lay across the threshold and we went past them, each with the same shudder of dread. There was only one old woman still squatting by the dead, some relation, talking to herself in an undertone. She bid me good-evening in a low voice, adding: *"A parahi oé!"* (Be seated).

Then I gazed on the face of the dead man, lighted up by the trembling flame of a native lamp. His eyes and mouth were half-open; his white beard seemed to have grown since his death; it was like a lichen on a brown stone; his long arms, all tattooed blue, had the rigid look of a mummy's limbs, and lay straight by his side; and that which struck me most of all in the dead face was the characteristic stamp of the Polynesian type, the Maori weirdness; altogether, the ideal image of the Toupapahou.

Rarahu's eyes had followed mine and fell on the dead; but she shivered and turned away. The poor little thing was determined not to be frightened; she was bent on staying to the end by the side of the old man who had shown her some kindness in her childhood. She had sincerely lamented the old woman Huamahine; but the rigid form before her had done nothing for her beyond leaving her to grow; she had no stronger feeling of attachment to him than those of respect and duty; his terrible corpse as it lay there filled her only with the extremest horror. The old watcher had fallen asleep. The rain was pouring in torrents on the trees, on the thatched roof, with strange noises of breaking branches and ominous cracking. The Toupapahous were abroad in the woods, crowding round us, peeping through every chink at this new hermit who had joined them since the morning. They might put their haggard hands in between the beams at any moment.

" Stay with me, my Loti," said Rarahu. " If you leave me, by to-morrow morning I shall be dead of fright...."

So there I stayed all night, holding her hand in mine; I kept her company till the first gleam of dawn began to peep between the bars of her dwelling. She had at last fallen asleep, her sweet little head, so sad and thin, resting on my shoulder. I laid her down gently on her mats and stole away. I knew that the Toupapahous vanish at the light of day and that I might now leave her in safety.

VII

LOTI AT HOME

Not far from the palace, behind the queen's gardens, in one of the quietest and greenest avenues of Papeete, was a fresh little bower standing by itself. It was built at the foot of a clump of such immensely tall coco-palms that it might have been taken for the microscopic dwelling of Lilliputians. On the side facing the road it had a verandah overgrown with the vanilla plant. Behind it was an enclosure, a perfect thicket of acacias, oleanders and hibiscus. Pink periwinkle grew everywhere in thick clumps, blossomed round the windows, and trailed into the rooms. There was shade all day in the little nook, and its peace was never disturbed.

There, a week after her adoptive father's death, Rarahu came to live with me. Her dream was crowned with fulfilment.

VIII

MUO FARE

One fine evening of the southern winter—the 12th of June, 1872—we held a grand reception. This was the *Muo Faré,* the house-warming, the consecration of the home. We gave a great *amurama*—supper and tea. Our guests were many, and two Chinese had been engaged in honour of the event, skilled in concocting subtleties in pastry with ginger, and in constructing towering pieces of confectionery of fantastic aspect.

Among the guests were, first and foremost, John, my brother John, who was seen at all the festivities in that strange land, but who remained a fascinating mystery quite inexplicable to the Tahitian damsels, who could never find the way to his heart, or the vulnerable point in his chaste nature. Then there were Plunket—known as Remuna—Prince Touin-vira, Pomaré's youngest son, and two other men known on board the *Reindeer*. And with these all the pleasure-loving train of the queen's ladies: Faïmana, Téria, Maramo, Raouréa, Tarahu, Eréré, Taouna, down to black Tétouara. Rarahu had got over her childish spite against all these women now that she was going to play mistress of the house and do the honours; just as Louis XII.,

King of France, forgot the grievances of the Duke of Orleans.

None of the guests failed to appear, and by eleven o'clock in the evening the little house was full of young women in muslin tunics crowned with flowers, and gaily drinking tea, syrups, or beer, munching sugar or cakes, and singing *himénés*.

In the course of the evening an incident occurred, really disastrous from the point of view of English decorum. Rarahu's big cat, brought that very morning from Apiré, which had been, as a precaution, shut into a cupboard, suddenly sprang out and on to the table—frightened out of its senses, yelling with terror, upsetting cups, and jumping out of the window. Its little mistress, embracing it fondly, restored it to the cupboard. Thus the catastrophe ended, and a few days later this very Turiri, completely tamed, had become quite a city cat of the best and most sociable manners.

At this Sardanapalesque supper Rarahu was already quite another creature. She wore a new dress, a *tapa* of white muslin with a train, which gave her quite a dignified air; and she did the honours with ease and grace, a little confused at times and then blushing deeply, but always charming.—I was complimented on her appearance; the women even, and Faïmana at their head, saying, " How pretty she is ! "

John, to be sure, was rather grave, but smiled at her all the same very benevolently. She was beaming with happiness; it was her introduction to the great world of women at Papeete, and so brilliant a début as her childish imagination had never dreamed of or wished for.

Thus lightly did she cross the fatal line. Poor wild-flower that had blossomed in the woods! She had been plunged, like so many others, into the unwholesome and artificial atmosphere in which she was fated to pine and fade.

IX

PEACEFUL TIMES

The days went by very gently under the towering coco-palms which shaded our dwelling.

To rise every morning soon after the sun, go past the boundary of the queen's garden, and there plunge into the stream that flows past the palace and take a long bath under the acacias—it was delicious in the pure fresh morning air of Tahiti! The bath, in fact, was spun out by easy chat with the women about the court, and carried us on till the midday meal. Rarahu's dinner was always extremely frugal; now, as at Apiré, she was content with baked bread-fruit and a few sweet cakes which the Chinese brought round for sale every morning.

Then sleep filled up the greater part of the day. Those who have lived in the tropics know the enervating luxury of that noon-day slumber. We hung up hammocks of New Zealand flax under the verandah and spent hours in them, dreaming or sleeping to the soothing chirp of the grasshoppers.

In the afternoon Téourahi would generally drop in to play cards with her friend Rarahu. Rarahu, who had begged to be taught écarté, had, like all the Tahitian women, a perfect passion for this European game; and the two young things, sitting opposite each other on a mat, would spend hours in absorbed interest, captivated by the thirty-two painted cards as they slipped through their fingers.

Then we had coral-fishing out on the reef. Rarahu and I would often go out on these excursions, in a native canoe, and would poke and grope in the warm blue water and fish up madrepores and cowries. Out in our un-gardened flower-plot, under the orange and gardenia shrubs, there were always shells to be seen drying, and corals bleaching in the sun, their delicate branches all tangled with creepers and pink periwinkle.

It was the same exotic, peaceful, sun-lit existence which my brother Rouéri had formerly led here, the life I had pictured and longed for in those strange dreams of my boyhood which had so constantly carried me to these distant lands of the sun. Time glided on, and all about me grew those thousand inextricable little threads, twined of the charms of the South Sea shores, which at last are knotted into a dangerous web, veiling the past, casting a shroud over home and our native land, till it has so closely enwrapped the dreamer that he cannot escape.

Rarahu was always singing. She could affect an endless variety of bird-like tones, some strident, some as soft as a linnet's note, and going up, up, to the highest pitch of the scale. She still was one of the leaders of the *himéné* choir of Apiré. From having spent her early years in the forest she had a great feeling for its contemplative and dreamy poetry; her original ideas she put into song. She improvised *himénés* whose wild and incoherent spirit would be quite unintelligible to any European if I tried to reproduce them. But to me these outlandish ditties had a singular, melancholy charm, especially when they came up softly on the deep silence of noon in Oceania.

Towards evening Rarahu very commonly prepared crowns to wear for the walk after dark. But they were not generally of her own devising. There were certain Chinese famous for composing the most extraordinary wreaths; they manufactured the strangest and most fantastic new forms of flowers by combining the leaves and petals of real flowers, mandarin's flowers indeed, with the stamp of artificial and Chinese prettiness. The flowers of the white gardenia, with its strong, heady scent, were always introduced in profusion in these singular towering wreaths, which were Rarahu's principal extravagance.

Another article of finery, more dressy than a crown of flowers, was the crown of *piia,* made of a fine white straw, like rice straw, plaited with wonderful skill and delicacy by the Tahitian women. Above the *piia* crown are placed bunches of *reva-reva* (a word meaning to float), which gave the finishing touch to this festal head-dress, fluttering like clouds at the lightest breath of air. *Reva-reva* is a knot of transparent and impalpable streamers of a golden-green colour, which the Tahitian women find in the heart of the coco-palm.

When it was dark, and Rarahu was dressed with her long hair unplaited down her back, we went out walking. We joined the crowd which wandered up in front of the illuminated booths of the Chinese shopkeepers in the high street of Papeete, or sat in a circle in the moonlight round the women dancing the Upa-Upa. But we always went home early, and Rarahu, who rarely took part in the amusements of her companions, had the reputation of being a very well-conducted little person. Then we had an hour of quiet enjoyment; still, it was not like those days of deep peace or light-hearted fun in the woods of Fataoua. There was something anxious and sad hanging over us. I loved her more than ever because she was alone in the world, and in the eyes of all Papeete she was my wife. The sweet habits of our domestic life bound us more closely day by day; and yet the life of this delightful to-day has no possible to-morrow; it must be cut short by separation and absence.

The most utter separation, which would put continents and oceans between us—the awful diameter of the whole earth !

X

It had been decided that we would go together to pay a visit to Tiahoui in her distant home; and Rarahu had looked forward to this excursion with joy for a long time. One fine morning we set out together, along the Faaa road, carrying our light baggage—Tahitian baggage is light—over our shoulders. A clean shirt for me, two *pareos* and a pink muslin *tapa* for Rarahu. In this happy land a man travels as he might have done in the mythical golden age, if travelling was invented in such remote times. The wanderer needs neither weapons, provisions nor money; hospitality is offered wherever he goes, cordial and gratuitous; and throughout the island there are no dangerous creatures excepting a few European colonists, and they are few and rare, centering for the most part near Papeete.

Our first halt was at Papara, which we reached at sunset, after walking all day. It was the hour when the native fishermen were coming in from the open in their frail outrigged canoes; the women of the place were awaiting them in groups on the strand, and our only difficulty was to choose whose offer we should accept, of a night's lodging. The slender craft ran on shore under the palms, one after another; the naked oarsmen beat the still waters with sweeping paddle-strokes, while they trumpeted loudly on their conch-shells like antique Tritons. It was amazingly original and vivid; simple and primitive, too, as a scene of the primeval world.

Next morning at daybreak we started again. The country about us now became grander and wilder. We crept along the shoulder of the mountain by the only path, whence we had a wide view over the vast expanse of ocean, with here and there a low islet covered with improbable-looking vegetation: pandanus of antediluvian aspect, and forests which might be relics of the extinct period of the Lias. A solemn leaden sky, like that of a past age, a shrouded sun dragging long shafts of pale silver over the wide waters. . . .

Here and there we came on a village hidden under palm-trees, oval cabins with thatched roofs, and grave Tahitians squatting about them half-asleep, dreaming their endless dreams; tattooed ancients, with the look of sphinxes and as motionless as stone —altogether an uncanny savagery, which transported my imagination to the dim unknown.

Strange is the fate of these Polynesian races, the forgotten leavings of a primitive people; there they remain, living in immobility and contemplation, gently dying out under the touch of civilized nations. —In another century their place will probably know them no more.

XI

Half-way on our road, in the district of Maraa, Rarahu had a shock of surprise and admiration.

We came upon a large grotto, opening like a church porch in the mountainside, and quite full of little birds. A colony of grey swallows had completely covered the rocky walls with their nests; startled by our visit they fluttered about in hundreds, vieing with each other in chirping and song.

In olden times these little creatures were believed by the Tahitians to be *varué*, spirits, departed souls; but even to Rarahu they were no more than a large family of birds; however, as she had never seen any before, they were also a new and delightful sight and she would have lingered long to watch them in an ecstasy, and imitate their notes. To her fancy the ideal land would be full of birds, where all day long they might be heard singing in the branches.

XII

A little distance before we reached the lands of the Papéuriri district, we came upon Téharo and Tiahoui, who had come out to meet us. Their joy at seeing us was sincere and noisy; a great display of glee when friends meet after absence is quite characteristic of the Tahitian.

These two worthy little savages were still in the first quarter of the honeymoon, a delightful season in Oceania as elsewhere, both very nice and hospitable in the widest acceptation of the word. Their hut was clean and neat, classic from the Tahitian point of view down to the smallest details. We found a large bed ready for us covered with white mats, and enclosed by native curtains made of the flattened and softened bark of the paper-mulberry.

High festival was held in our honour at Papéuriri and we spent a few delightful days there. The evenings indeed, were strangely dismal; in the darkness I felt the solitude and wildness of this out-of-the-way world. At night, when I heard far away the sounds of the plaintive reed-pipes, or the lugubrious hollow trump of the conch-shells, I felt how fearfully far I was from home, and a strange ruefulness weighed on my heart.

Tiahoui gave some grand banquets for us, to which the whole village was invited; menus of the choicest character—little pigs baked whole underground, and delicious fruits to follow; and dancing and *himénes* in chorus, charmingly sung.

I had started on this journey in Tahitian undress, my feet and legs bare, and my whole wardrobe a clean white shirt and the national *pareo* or loincloth. There was nothing to prevent my taking myself for a native; and now and then I caught myself wishing I really were to the manner born; I envied our friends their peaceful happiness. Here, too, in her native atmosphere, Rarahu was herself again, more natural and even more charming; she was the laughing little maid of the waterfall once more, in all her bewitching simplicity.

Now for the first time I began to think that there would be a peculiar satisfaction in going to live with her for my little wife in some very remote district, or one of the furthest and least known of the islands of Pomaré's realm; in being forgotten by all, and dead to all the world; in keeping her as she was, as I had loved her—so unique and savage with all her innate innocence and ignorance.

XIII

A wonderful year for Papeete was 1872. Never had there been so many fêtes, dances and *amuramas*.

Every evening it was a bewildering scene. At nightfall the Tahitian damsels decked themselves with gorgeous flowers; rapid beating on the tom-tom bid them all collect for the *upa-upa*. They all rushed at the call, their hair flying, their figures scarcely veiled by the thin muslin tunic, and the dancing, wildly suggestive, lasted sometimes till daybreak.

Pomaré winked at these old-world saturnalia, which a certain governor vainly attempted to prohibit; they amused the little princess, who was dying by inches in spite of all that could be done to check the disease, and anything was acceptable which could divert her thoughts.

These entertainments, where every woman of Papeete was to be seen, commonly took place in front of the palace terrace. The queen and the princesses would all come out and look on with superior indifference, reclining on mats in the moonlight. The dancers clapped their hands and sang in chorus to the tom-tom with frenzied rapidity. Each in turn danced a figure; the step and the music, slow at first, presently increased to a delirious pace, and when the exhausted dancer suddenly stopped, at loud rattle on the drums, another sprang forward to take her place and outdo her in fury and indecency. The girls of the Pomotous isles were a separate and even wilder group, and vied with those of Tahiti. Wearing enormous wreaths of datura and their hair towzled like mad creatures, they danced to a shorter and more abrupt rhythm, but charmingly too, so that it was hard to say which one preferred.

Rarahu was passionately addicted to these performances which fired the blood, but she never danced. She dressed herself out like the rest, wore a wreath of rare flowers, and let the heavy masses of her hair fall over her shoulders; and then, for hours together, she would sit by my side on the palace steps, absorbed and silent.

We went home again with our heads turned, intoxicated as it were by the noise, and alive to all sorts of new sensations. Rarahu was then like another creature. The *upa-upa* stirred the savage in her untrained soul.

XIV

Rarahu wore the costume of the island, the flowing, waistless tunics known as *tapa*. She wore hers long and trailing, with almost European elegance. She could already distinguish a new shape or cut of the sleeves or body, and certain pretty or ugly fashions. She was already a civilized and coquettish little lady.   In the day-time she wore a broadbrimmed hat of fine white Tahitian straw, tilted forward over her eyes; on the crown, which was low like that of a sailor's hat, she would put a wreath of natural leaves or flowers. She had grown fairer in the shade, and living the town-life; and many a brown-bosomed Andalusian would have looked darker than my little Tahitian. But for the slight tattoo marks on her forehead, which her companions laughed at and I thought pretty, she would have passed for a white-skin. But still, in certain lights, her skin was shot, as it were, with a rosy-copper hue, an exotic tinge which betrayed the Maori race in its affinity with the red-skin Indians of America.

In the world of Papeete she asserted herself with more and more decisiveness as Loti's well-conducted and undeniable little wife, and even at government house the queen as she shook hands with me would say: " Well, and how is Rarahu? "

In the street she attracted attention, and new-comers in the colony, as she passed them, would ask her name; even at first sight everyone was charmed by that expressive look, that delicate profile and beautiful hair.

She was more of a woman, too, her perfect figure was fuller and rounder, but now and again a pale blue cloud marked the orbits of her eyes, and a little dry cough, like that of the queen's children, shook her chest from time to time.

In her mind a great and rapid change was going on, and I could hardly keep pace with the development of her intelligence. She was already so far civilized as to like my calling her a little savage, to understand that this had its charm for me, and she would gain nothing by aping the ways of white women. She read her Bible a great deal, and the glorious promises of the Gospel sent her into raptures; she had her hours of ardent and mystical faith. Her nature was full of contradictions; the most antagonistic feelings dwelt there in wild confusion; she was never the same creature two days running.

She was, even now, scarcely fifteen, and her notions on all subjects were mistaken and childish;

her extreme youth gave bewitching charm to this incoherency of ideas and conceptions.

God knows that within the limits of my weak faith I guided her lovingly towards all that I believed to be good and true. God knows that not a word or a doubt on my part ever shook her innocent confidence in eternity and the Redemption. . . .

My brother John spent part of his day with us; a few European friends from the *Reindeer,* or belonging to the European colony, often came to see us in our peaceful home; they were very happy under our roof. Most of them could not speak Tahitian, but Rarahu's childlike voice and happy smile attracted those who did not understand her tongue. All loved her and regarded her as a person apart from her fellows, having a right to the same consideration as a white woman.

XV

I had long been able to talk " 'Long shore " Tahitian, which is to pure Tahitian what " little nigger " talk is to French; but I now began to express myself in the correct language and whimsical forms of the old tongue, and Pomaré would hold long conversations with me. There were two persons who could understand me and help in my studies of a speech which is fast becoming extinct: Rarahu and the queen.

The queen, indeed, in the course of long games of écarté, would instruct me with great interest, delighted to find that I cared to learn and loved this dying, if not dead, language. I, for my part, took pleasure in questioning her as to the legends, customs and traditions of the past. She spoke slowly, in a low, husky voice, and from her I learnt strange things, old-world tales of the remote, mysterious and forgotten times which the Polynesians speak of as " The Night." The word *Po* in Tahitian signifies the night and darkness, and also the legendary part which even the old folks cannot remember.

XVI

THE LEGEND OF THE POMOTOUS AS NARRATED BY QUEEN POMARE

" The Pomotous islands—Isles of the Night, or subject islands—which we now call Tuamotous— far off Isles—by the desire of their chiefs, are still partly inhabited, as you know, by poor cannibals. They were the last to be peopled of all our island groups. They were formerly guarded by the water-fiends, who beat the sea so hard with their great albatross-wings that no one could get near them. But the spirits were beaten and destroyed very long ago by the god Taaroa.

" After their defeat the first Maoris were able to land and people the Pomotous."

XVII

THE LEGEND OF THE MOONS

" The Oceanian legend tells that of old there were five moons in the sky over the Great Ocean. They had human faces, much more plain to see than that of the present moon, and cast malignant spells on the first men who inhabited Tahiti; those who looked up at them were taken with a strange madness.

" The great god Taaroa went forth to destroy their power. Then they were much excited; they might be heard singing together in the infinite, with great, far-away, terrible voices; they sang magic songs as they went away, away, from the earth. But under Taaroa's power they began to tremble, and turned giddy, and fell with a noise of thunder into the sea which boiled and opened to swallow them.

" These five moons as they fell made the islands of Bora-Bora, Emeo, Huahine, Raïatéa, and Toubouai-Manou."

XVIII

Prince Tamatoa was sitting near me under the palace verandah. It was a short while before the horrible scenes which led to his being shut up again in the prison of Taravao. On his knees sat his pale little daughter, Pomaré V., whom he was gently caressing with his great, terrible hands. And the old queen looked at them with an expression of infinite tenderness and unspeakable sadness.

The little princess, too, was very sad; she held a dead bird in her hand and was gazing with tearful eyes at an empty cage. It was a singing-bird, a rare creature in Tahiti; it had been brought to her from America and the possession of it had given her the greatest joy.

" Loti," said she, " the white-haired admiral tells us that your ship is soon going to the land of California (*i te fenua California*). When you come back again I want you to bring me a very great quantity of birds, a great cage quite full; and I will let them fly in the woods of Fataoua, so that by the time when I am big, there will be singing-birds in our country as there are in others. . . . ."

XIX

In the island of Tahiti, life is localized by the seashore; the villages are scattered along the strand and the centre is a wilderness.

The interior is uninhabited, and overgrown with dense forests, a wild region broken by ramparts of inaccessible peaks where eternal silence reigns. In the valleys, curiously imbedded in the heart of the island, nature is gloomy but impressive; towering cliffs rise far above the tree-tops, and sharp peaks cut the sky-line. One could fancy oneself at the foot of a fantastic cathedral, its spires catching the clouds as they fleet past—all the little wandering cloudlets which the trade-winds sweep up from the ocean are impaled as they fly over; they are piled up against the basalt wall to fall in dew or gather into rills and waterfalls. Warm rain and dense mists keep these ravines perennially fresh and green, with strange mosses and amazing ferns.

Falling, as it were, to meet the cascades of Hyde Park and the Bois de Boulogne, the waters of Fataoua tumbling towards our old world break the deep peaceful silence of nature by their monotonous roar. It was at about eleven thousand yards above the deserted lodge where Huamahine and Tahaapaïru had lived, climbing up the stream through brakes and over rocks, that we came on the waterfall, which is famous throughout the islands, and which Tiahoui and Rarahu had often taken me to see.

We had not been there again, however, since settling at Papeete, so, in September, we made it the goal of an expedition which left its mark on our memories.

On our way Rarahu wished first to stop at the hut where her old parents had lived; she went in, holding me by the hand, and under the thatched roof, already falling in, she gazed speechlessly at the various familiar objects which time and men as yet had spared. In this house, standing wide open, nothing had been touched since the day when Tahaapaïru's body had been borne out. The wooden chests were in their place, the clumsy seats, the mats and the native lamp hanging to the wall; Rarahu had carried nothing away but the big Bible that had belonged to the old folks.

Then we went on our way further into the valley, along shady and overgrown paths, true forest paths in a virgin land, sunk between the rocks. After walking for about an hour we heard the loud hollow plunge of the waters close at hand. We had reached the foot of the dark ravine, where the torrent of Fataoua falls with a sheer leap of more than nine hundred feet, like a great silver sheaf.

In the depths of this gorge the scene was one of pure enchantment. The most lavish vegetation grew tangled in the shade, dripping and revelling in the perpetual deluge; creepers clung to the steep, black walls, and among them grew tree-ferns, mosses and exquisite varieties of maiden-hair. The water from above, pulverized to dust in its fall came down like a torrent of rain, a rush of furious, dishevelled drops. It collected below, foaming fiercely in the basins it had hollowed in the rock smoothed by the patient hand of ages; and then danced away in a stream again, pursuing its way under the greenery.

A fine dust of water hung like a veil over all, and just overhead appeared the sky, as if seen from the bottom of a well, and the heads of the cliffs half-hidden in dark clouds.

What most struck Rarahu was this perennial stir in the heart of such utter solitude, this great noise without life—nothing but inert nature following, during incalculable ages, the impulse given at the creation.

We turned off to the left by goat-paths which zig-zagged up the mountain side. We walked under a thick vault of foliage; among trees of ancient growth whose moist greenish trunks, towering above us, gleamed like enormous columns of polished marble. Climbers hung in garlands on all sides, and tree-ferns spread their wide parasols, cut and fringed like the finest lace. Still climbing, we came upon clumps of rose-bushes and whole thickets of roses in bloom. The China-rose grew on these heights in astonishing profusion, and in the moss at our feet was a perfect carpet of fragrant wood-strawberry—it might have been a fairy-garden.

Rarahu had never been so far; and a sort of vague alarm came over her as we went deeper and deeper into the wilderness. The Tahitian women are indolent and rarely venture into the heart of the island, which is as much a *terra incognita* to them as any distant land. The men, even, scarcely visit these solitudes. Some now and then come up to gather wild bananas or cut some precious wood. But it was so lovely that she was enchanted. She made herself a crown of roses and laughed as she tore her dress on the thorns by the way.

What most delighted us wherever we went were the ferns, which spread their huge fronds with matchless delicacy of outline and variety of tender hues.

Thus, all day we went upwards, towards the lonely regions where no human path could be discerned; here and there deep gorges opened at our feet—black jagged rents in the mountain-side; the air grew crisper and colder, and we came to great clouds with sharp, dark edges, which seemed to lie asleep leaning against the rocky wall, some above our heads, and others below our feet.

XX

By the evening we had almost reached the central highland of Tahiti;—far below us through the transparent air we could see the outline of all the volcanic ruin, and the mountains in relief; enormous ribs of basalt, starting from the crater in the middle, and sinking gradually till they were lost in the waves. All round, the blue ocean, and the horizon so high that, by a common optical illusion, the expanse of water had a strange appearance of being concave. The ocean-line lay far above the highest peaks; Oroena alone, the giant of the Tahitian system, cut it with its dark majestic head. All round the island a belt of white spray lay on the blue expanse of the Pacific; the line of the barrier reef where eternal surf beats on the coral shoal.

Quite in the distance lay the little isle of Toubouaimanou, and the island of Moorea; puffs of cloud of unimaginable hues floated over their blue summits, hanging as it seemed in the limitless vault.

From that height we looked down on this grand panorama of Oceanian nature, as though we ourselves were no longer of this world. It was so sublimely beautiful that we sat in ecstasy side by side on a boulder, without speaking a word.

" Loti," said Rarahu, after a long silence, " what are your thoughts? "

" Of many things," said I, " which you cannot understand. I am thinking, my little pet, that on those distant seas are scattered many unknown islands; that they are inhabited by a mysterious race destined soon to perish; that you are a child of this primitive race; and that here, perched on the summit of one of these islands, far from all human creatures in this absolute solitude, I, a son of the old world, born on the other side of the globe, am sitting and loving you.

" Long ago, Rarahu, very long ago, before the first men were born, the mighty hand of Atua raised these hills from out of the sea; the island of Tahiti, as hot as red-hot iron, came up like a storm, in the midst of flames and smoke. Then the first rain which fell to refresh the earth after these terrors, traced the way which the Fataoua brook follows to this day through the forest.

" All the great features you see are everlasting; they will still be the same hundreds of ages hence, when the Maori race will long since have vanished to be no more than a dim memory preserved in the books of a bygone day."

" There is one thing that frightens me, O Loti, my beloved," said she. " How did the first Maoris get here, since nowadays they have no boats big enough to trade with the islands beyond their own group? How did they come from that far-away land where, as the Bible tells us, the first man was created? Our race is so different from yours that I am frightened lest, in spite of all that missionaries say, your saving God should not have come down for us, and should refuse to know us. . . ."

The sun, which was about to rise on an autumn morning in Europe, was sinking fast in our sky and shedding its last golden rays on the gigantic scenery at our feet. The heavy mists which slept in the ravines of the basalt assumed strange coppery hues; on the horizon the island of Moorea glowed like living fire, its tall peaks were orange flame, and dazzling with splendour.

And suddenly all the great blaze went out; and night fell swiftly, with no twilight, and the Southern Cross and all the austral stars shone out against the deep sky.

" Loti," said Rarahu, " how high should we have to climb to catch sight of your country? "

XXI

When it was quite dark Rarahu, as I need not say, was afraid.

The silence of that night was indeed like nothing on earth. The breakers, far below us, were too distant to be heard; there was not even a crackle in the branches, not a whisper of leaves; the atmosphere was absolutely still. Such silence is unknown save in these deserted solitudes where there is not even a bird.

All about us there were still dim phantoms of trees and ferns, as if we were down in the familiar groves of Fataoua; but by the pale light of the stars we had transient glimpses of the giddy blue hollow of the sea beneath; we were in the grip as it were of this sublime immensity and solitude.

Tahiti is one of the few countries where one may safely go to sleep in the woods on a bed of dry leaves and fern, with a loin-cloth for a coverlet. And this we presently did—after carefully seeking an open spot where there was no fear of being seized by Toupapahous. Though, indeed, these ill-omened prowlers of the night, haunting by preference spots where human beings have dwelt, do not climb so high or visit virgin regions such as that where we lay down to rest.

I lay awake a long time, musing as I gazed at the sky. Stars, and more stars; myriads of radiant sparks in the wondrous blue depths above; all the constellations unknown to Europe, slowly circling round the Southern Cross.

Rarahu, too, was lost in contemplation, her eyes wide open, and speaking not a word; she alternately looked at me, with a smile, and stared up at the sky. The grand nebulae of the southern hemisphere flickered like broad smears of phosphorus, and between them lay vacant spaces, huge black pits, in which no cosmic dust could be discerned, and which suggested to the fancy apocalyptic and fearful notions of the immense void.

Suddenly a terrifying black bulk came slowly rolling down from Oroena and on to us. It was of the most extraordinary shape, sinister and ominous of aspect. In one instant it had wrapped us in such total darkness that we could not see each other. A gust swept past, covering us with leaves and dead twigs, and at the same moment a torrent of rain drenched us with icy-cold water.

Feeling our way, we groped till we found the trunk of a great tree, against which we leaned for shelter, clinging very closely together, both of us quaking with cold, and she from fear too—a little.

When this squall was past day was breaking, driving clouds and ghosts before it. We dried our clothes in the brilliant sunshine, laughing as we did so, and after a very frugal Tahitian meal, made our way down the mountain again.

XXII

In the evening we had reached the foot of Fataoua once more, dreadfully tired and desperately hungry, but without any further adventure.

There we met two young men unknown to us, who had come in from the woods. Their raiment was the national *pareo* knotted about their loins; on their way through the rose-brake they had made thick garlands for their heads, like Rarahu's, and the fruits they had gathered they carried at the end of long sticks resting on their bare shoulders—fine bread-fruit and wild bananas, red and orange. With them we encamped in a delightful dell under a bower of lemon-tres in bloom.

A flame, produced by rubbing two dry branches

together, was soon flickering under their hands; a large fire was made, and the fruits baked in the ashes made an excellent meal, of which the two youths gladly offered us half, as is the custom in those parts.

Rarahu had brought home from this excursion as many amazing and exciting experiences as if she had made a voyage to some foreign land. Her childlike intelligence had unfolded to a variety of new ideas on the vastness and the structure of the universe, on the distribution of human races, and the mystery of their destiny.

XXIII

Two very elegant young persons at Papeete were Rarahu and her friend Téourahi, setting the fashion to other young women in the matter of new colours in dresses, or certain flowers or certain shapes in wreaths. They generally went barefoot, poor little things, and their luxury, which consisted chiefly in crowns of fresh roses, was of a very humble kind. But the grace and youth of their faces, the perfect and classic mould of their figures gave them an air of ample adornment even with these simple aids, and made them quite bewitching.

They often went on the sea in a slender canoe with outriggers, which they managed themselves, and they loved to come laughing by under the bows of the *Reindeer*. When they hoisted a sail their fragile bark, laid on her beam-ends by the steady trade-wind, flew at a wonderful pace; and they, standing up, with sparkling eyes and floating hair, skimmed over the water like phantoms. They had the art of trimming the balance of the arrow-like boat in which they shot past by slight movements of the body—and they were gone, leaving a long wake of white foam.

XXIV

> "Delicious Tahiti, a Polynesian queen, an European island in the bosom of the savage ocean; the pearl and diamond of that fifth world."—DUMONT D'URVILLE.

The scene took place at Queen Pomaré's palace in November, 1872.

The court, which commonly goes barefoot, lying on the fresh grass or on mats of pandanus fibre, was in full dress that evening, keeping high festival.

I was at the piano; before me was the score of the "*Africaine*." This piano, which had only that morning arrived, was a novelty at the court of Tahiti; it was a costly instrument with a soft, rich tone, like the notes of an organ or of distant bells, and Meyerbeer's music was to be heard for the first time in the halls of Pomaré. Standing by me was my shipmate Randle, who subsequently left the sea to become a leading tenor in the American opera houses; he enjoyed a brief spell of fame under the name of Randetti, until, having taken to drink, he died in abject poverty.

He was just now in full possession of his voice and gifts, and never have I heard a man's voice more touching or more exquisite. He and I together charmed many Tahitian ears, for in that land music is instinctively understood by all, even by the most savage natives.

At the upper end of the room, under a full-length portrait of herself—painted by a clever artist some thirty years before, and representing her as handsome and idealized—sat the old queen on her gilt throne, which was covered with red brocade. In her arms was her now dying grandchild, little Pomaré V., who fixed her large black eyes, glittering with fever, on my face. The old woman's ungraceful bulk filled the whole breadth of her seat. She was dressed in a loose gown of crimson velvet, a stockingless ankle was laced in slipshod fashion into a satin boot. By the side of the throne was a tray full of pandanus cigarettes.

An interpreter in evening-dress stood close at hand, for this woman, who understood French as well as any Parisian, never in her life would utter a single word of it.

The admiral, the governor, and the consuls had seats near Her Majesty.

There still was dignity in that face, brown, wrinkled, set and hard as it was; above all else it was sad, infinitely sad—with watching as death snatched from her all her children, one after another, all stricken with the same incurable malady; with seeing her kingdom invaded by civilization and fast breaking up, her lovely island degraded to a scene of debauchery.

The windows were open to the gardens, and outside heads could be seen crowned with flowers, and moving to and fro as they came closer to hear. All the women in attendance on the queen; Faïmana, wreathed like a naiad with water-plants and reeds; Téhamana with a crown of datura, Téria, Raouréa, Tapou, Eréré, Taïréa, Tiahoui and Rarahu.

The side of the room opposite to where I sat was all open; there was no wall, only a colonnade of timber, and beyond it the Tahitian landscape under a star-sown sky.

At the feet of the columns, against that dark, remote background, rose a whole row of figures seated on a bench; the ladies of rank these, princesses or chiefs in their own right. Four gilt candelabra of Pompadour style, astonished at finding themselves amid such surroundings, lighted them fully and showed off their dresses, which were really very elegant and handsome. Their feet, naturally small, were neatly shod in irreproachable satin boots.

Here was the splendid Ariinoore, in a tunic of cherry-coloured satin and a garland of *péia*— Ariinoore, who refused to marry Lieutenant M——, of the French navy, though he had ruined himself in buying her a *corbeille*,—and who had also rejected Kaméhaméha V., king of the Sandwich Islands.

By her side sat Paüra, her inseparable friend, a fascinating type of savage with her singular ugliness—or beauty? A head that would eat raw fish or human flesh—a strange creature, dwelling in the forest wilds of a remote district, with the education of an English Miss—waltzing, too, like a Spaniard.

Then Titaüa, who charmed Prince Alfred of England, the only Tahitian who ever preserved any beauty in her riper years; she was a constellation of splendid pearls and crowned with fluttering *réva-réva*. Her two daughters, just come home from a school in London, were as handsome as their mother. They wore European ball-dresses, half-disguised out of regard for the queen's prejudices, under Tahitian *tapas* of white gauze.

Princess Ariitéa, Pomaré's daughter-in-law, with her sweet, innocent, dreamy face, faithful to her own head-dress of China-roses caught here and there in her flowing hair.

The queen of Bora-Bora, a thorough old savage with pointed teeth, in a velvet dress.

Queen Moé (Moé meaning sleep or mystery) in a dark robe; regular features and a mystical type of face, with strange eyes half-shut, and an expression of introspection, like some old-fashioned portraits.

Behind these groups, in broad candle-light, rose the mountain peaks, dark in the transparent atmosphere of the Oceanian night, sharply outlined against the starry sky; and in the foreground the picturesque mass of a clump of bananas with their enormous leaves and bunches of fruit, looking like colossal candelabra ending in great black flowers. As a background to these trees the nebulae of the southern hemisphere spread a sheet of blue light, and in the middle blazed the Southern Cross. Nothing could be more ideally tropical than this far-away perspective.

The air was full of that exquisite fragrance of orange-blossom and gardenia which is distilled by night under the thick foliage; there was a great silence, accenuated by the bustle of insects in the grass, and that sonorous quality, peculiar to night in Tahiti, which predisposes the listener to feel the enchanting power of music.

The piece we chose was Vasco's song when he walks alone in the island he has just discovered, intoxicated with admiration for its strange new aspect—a passage in which the composer has perfectly represented all he knew by intuition of the remote glories of these lands of light and verdure. And Randle, with a glance at the scene around him, began in his lovely voice :

   " Land of wondrous beauty, gardens of delight

   . . . .

   O Paradise !—risen from the waters ! "

   . . . .

The shade of Meyerbeer must have felt a thrill of pleasure that evening, at hearing his music thus rendered at the other side of the world.

XXV

Towards the close of the year a grand festival was to be held in the island of Moorea, on the occasion of the consecration of the church at Afareahitu.

Queen Pomaré expressed to the white-haired admiral her intention of being present with all her suite, and invited him also to the ceremony, and to the banquet which was to follow. The admiral placed his ship at Her Majesty's disposal, and it was agreed that the *Reindeer* should get under way and carry all the court.

Pomaré's suite was numerous, noisy and picturesque; it was increased, too, in honour of the occasion by a reinforcement of two or three hundred damsels, who had spent fortunes in *réva-réva* and flowers.

One fine clear morning in December the *Reindeer*, having unreefed her white sails, was taken by storm by this gleeful mob.

I had been told off to go in full uniform and escort the queen from the palace. She, wishing to embark with no display of ceremony, had sent the women before her, and we, her little private party, made our way together down to the beach in the first gleam of sunrise.

The old queen led the way in a red dress, leading her darling grandchild by the hand, and we followed close behind—Princess Ariitéa, Queen Moé, the queen of Bora-Bora and I.

The picture often recurs in my reminiscences. Most women have their hours of brightest radiancy; and the image of Ariitéa, walking by my side, under the exotic trees, in the broad level morning light, is the one I still see whenever I think of her across all those leagues, those years.

As soon as the captain's launch came alongside of the *Reindeer,* bringing the queen and the princesses on board, the ship's crew, manning the yards with the usual ceremony, gave three cheers for Queen Pomaré, and one-and-twenty discharges of cannon echoed along the quiet shores of Tahiti. The queen and court then withdrew to the admiral's room, where a breakfast was prepared for them, after their taste, of bonbons and fruits washed down with old champagne.

The following, meanwhile, had invaded every part of the ship, where they were having a high time, pelting the sailors with oranges, bananas and flowers.

Rarahu, too, was on board, one of the royal suite; pensive, she, and serious in the midst of all this noisy fun. Pomaré had taken with her the best *himéné* choirs of the island, and Rarahu, who was one of the chief singers of the Apiré district, had, consequently, found herself included.

A digression is here needed to explain what is meant by the *tiaré miri,* an object which has no equivalent in the accessories of the toilet of European women. The *tiaré* is a sort of green, dahlia-like flower, which the women of Oceania wear in their hair, just over the ear, on high holidays. On examining this strange-looking flower it is seen to be artificially composed; the stem is a twig of rush, and the flower is made of the leaves of a very fragrant little parasitical plant, a kind of lycopodium, which grows on certain forest trees. The Chinese excel in manufacturing artistic *tiarés,* which they sell very dear to the girls of Papeete.

The *tiaré* is their special adornment for festivals, banquets and dances, and its presentation to a man is equivalent to throwing the handkerchief.

Now, on this occasion all the Tahitian women wore *tiarés* in their hair.

Ariitéa had commanded me to attend her and keep her amused during the ceremonial breakfast, and poor little Rarahu, who had come only for my sake, sat a long while on the deck waiting for me, and shedding silent tears at finding herself thus deserted. A severe punishment for a childish whim which had lasted since the day before and had already cost her many tears.

XXVI

The crossing had taken about two hours, and we were now close to the island of Moorea. There was a great deal of noise in the officers' room of the *Reindeer;* about a dozen of young women, chosen from among the prettiest and the most popular, had been invited to a luncheon by the officers.

In my absence Rarahu had accepted an invitation to join the party. She was there with Téourahi and some other friends; she had dried her tears and was in fits of laughter. She could not speak French, and most of the others did; but by signs and monosyllables she kept up animated communications with her neighbours, who thought her charming.

Finally—the crowning act of perfidy and baseness —at dessert she had, with many graces, offered her *tiaré* to Plunket.

She was sharp enough, to be sure, to know exactly what she was about; and that Plunket certainly would not accept her meaning.

XXVII

What words could paint that scene of enchantment, the bay of Afareahitu!

Great black bluffs of fantastic outlines, dense, untrodden forests; mysterious screens of coco-palms bending over the placid water; and under the tall trees a few scattered huts among groves of orange and oleander.

At first sight one might fancy that there were no inhabitants of this shady land; but in fact the whole population of Moorea were silently awaiting us, half-hidden under the vault of verdure.

In these woods the air is fresh and moist, with a strange aroma of exotic mosses and flowers; all the *himéné* choirs of Moorea were there, sitting in good order among the giant tree-trunks; all the singers of each district wearing the same colour, some white, others green or pink; all the women were crowned with flowers, all the men with leaves or reeds. A few groups, shyer or more savage, lurked in the background under the wood, and watched us as we came, half-hidden behind the trees.

The queen disembarked with the same ceremony as had been observed when she went on board, and the roar of the guns rolled away to the hills. She set foot on shore and walked on, led by the admiral. The times are past when the islanders would have carried her in their arms for fear her foot should touch the soil; the old prerogative by which any spot of earth trodden on by the queen became the property of the crown has long since been forgotten in Oceania.

A score of mounted lancers, Pomaré's whole guard of honour, were drawn up on the strand to receive her. As soon as she appeared all the choirs sang together the traditional chant " *Ia ora na oe, Pomaré vahine!* "—" Hail to thee, Queen Pomaré ! " —and the woods rang with shouts. It was as though we had landed on an enchanted island which had suddenly waked up at the touch of a magic wand.

XXVIII

The ceremony of consecrating the church at Afareahitu was a long one. The missionaries preached long sermons in Tahitian, and the *himénés* sang psalms of joy in praise of the Almighty. The building was of coral rock; the roof, thatched with pandanus-leaves, was constructed of large beams bound together by cords of various colours, in the old Maori style of architecture. I can see the quaint scene now—the doors of the church wide open to the country, a lovely landscape of hills and tall palms;—the queen close to the missionary's pulpit, in a black robe, praying for her grandchild, and by her side her old friend the chieftainess of Papara. All about her the women in her train in white tunics. The whole church was filled with heads crowned with flowers—and in the crowd was Rarahu, whom I had left to come off the *Reindeer* as though she were a stranger.

There was solemn silence when the Apiré choir,

which had been reserved till the last, began to sing a hymn, and I could distinguish my little friend's voice behind me, pure and strong above the rest. Under an impulse of religious excitement, or of passion, she warbled the most vehement and fantastic variations; her voice rang out like the ring of a crystal in the silence of the church, where she captivated the attention of all.

XXIX

After the service we went into the banqueting hall. The tables were laid in fact in the open air, under awnings of foliage, among the coco-palms. Five or six hundred persons were accommodated; the table-cloths were covered with lace-like leaves and amaranth-flowers. There were great decorative erections contrived by the Chinese out of banana stems and various singular plants. Side by side with European dishes there was an abundance of native messes: pastes of dried fruit, little pigs baked whole, and shrimps fermented in milk. Sauces were served in canoes, which the bearers had no small difficulty in carrying round. The chiefs, men and women alike, took it in turn to harangue the queen at the top of their voices, so loud, and with such vehemence, that they might have been taken for possessed creatures. Those who could not find room at the tables, ate standing, resting their plates on the shoulders of those who were seated;—the hubbub and confusion defy description.

I, sitting with the princesses, affected to pay no

heed to Rarahu, who was a long way off among the crowd, with the party from Apiré.

XXX

When night fell on the woods of Afareahitu the queen went to the *Farehaü* of the district, where a lodging had been made ready for her. The " White-haired Admiral " returned on board his frigate, and the *upa-upa* began.

Every thought of religion, every Christian feeling had fled with the daylight; the soft sensual dark-ness came down on the savage land, as in the time when its first discoverers had called it the New Cythera.

And I went off to the *Reindeer* with the admiral, leaving Rarahu on shore with that wild crew.

XXXI

On board, when I was alone, I sadly went on deck. The frigate, in the morning so full of life, was silent and deserted; the masts and yards pro-jected their rigid outline against the dark sky, the stars were dimmed, the air was thick and heavy, the sea dull and still. The bluffs of Moorea cast their black shadows upside down on the water; in the distance gleamed the bonfires, lighting up the savage dance; hoarse sounds of foul songs floated off in a confused murmur to the accompaniment of tom-toms beaten out of time.

I was filled with remorse at having left her to her fate amid this saturnalia; an uneasy dejection kept me up, with my eyes fixed on those fires on the strand; the sounds wafted from the land went to my heart. All the hours of the night struck one after another, on board the *Reindeer,* and sleep never came to put an end to my weird watch. I was very fond of the poor little thing, and the Tahitians always called her Loti's little wife. She was to all intent my little wife; I loved her truly. And yet there was a great gulf between us—a great gate for ever shut. She was a little savage; between us two who were one flesh there was the radical difference of race and utter divergence of views on the first elements of things. If my ideas and conceptions were often impenetrably dark to her, so were hers to me; my childhood, my native land, my home and hearth would for ever remain to her incomprehensible and strange. I remembered what she had once said to me: " I am afraid lest the same God did not create us both." In truth we were the offspring of two types of nature absolutely apart and dissimilar, and the union of our souls could only be brief, imperfect and stormy.

Poor little Rarahu ! Very soon, when we are so very far asunder, you will lapse into a little Maori girl again, to remain so, ignorant and wild; you will die in your far-away island, alone and forgotten— and Loti will perhaps not even know of it ! . . . . .

By this time a scarcely perceptible outline was beginning to show in the offing; it was the island of Tahiti. The sky was growing pale in the east, the fires on shore were dying out, the songs were silenced. And I could not help thinking of Rarahu, at this hour of the morning, tired out with dancing and left to herself. The idea scorched me like a hot iron.

XXXII

In the afternoon the queen and princesses came on board again to return to Papeete. When they had been received with the customary honours I stood watching the swarm of little barks, native canoes and fishing boats, which were bringing off her suite, the crowd being swelled by a number of women from Moorea, who wished to continue the revels at Tahiti. At last I descried Rarahu; she, too, was homeward-bound. She had changed her white *tapa* for a pink one, and put fresh flowers in her hair; she looked sad and absent-minded; her face was pale; the tattoo marks stood out on her pallid brow, and the blue rings round her eyes were darker than usual. She had danced till morning no doubt; but she was here, she had come back to me, and for the moment that was all I asked of her.

XXXIII

The return passage was perfectly calm and fine. Evening fell, the sun had sunk, the ship glided noiselessly on, leaving a furrow of broad slow waves which parted and rolled away to die in a sea as unruffled as glass. Large, dark clouds hung here and there in the sky, in sharp contrast to the pale yellow tint of evening, in the marvellously translucent atmosphere.

A group of young women in the after part of the ship showed in graceful silhouette against the sea and fading landscape. The party surprised me greatly: Ariitéa and Rarahu talking together like old friends, and with them Maramo, Faïmana and two other ladies-in-waiting on the queen. They were discussing a *himéné* composed by Rarahu, which she had just taught them, and which they were about to sing together. Presently they began —a new song in three parts—Ariitéa, Rarahu and Maramo. Rarahu's voice, clear above the others, gave out these words very distinctly, and not one of them was lost on me :

—" Heahaa noa iho (e) ! te tara no Paia (e) i tou nei tai ia oe, tau hoa (e) ! ehahe ! . . .

—" Ua iriti hoi au (e) ! i te tumu no te tiare, ei faaite i tau tai ia oe, tau hoa (e) ! ehahe ! . . .

—" Ua taa tau hoa (e) ! ei Farani te fenua, e neva oe to mata, aita e hio hoi au (e) ! ehahe ! . . ."

ROUGH TRANSLATION :

" Less than my grief for you is the top of Paia (the great tor of Bora-Bora), oh my love ! Alas !

" And I have torn out the *tiaré* by the roots to show my grief for you, oh my love ! Alas !

" You are gone, my love, to the land of France;

you will look up towards me, but never shall I see you more! Alas!"

This chant which rang out mournfully in the evening over the vast Pacific, with its strange rhythm sung by the three women's voices, is indelibly graven on my memory, and is one of the acutest reminiscences of Polynesia left on my mind. ...

XXXIV

It was quite dark by the time the noisy rout reached Papeete, where they were met by a great crowd. In a moment we had found each other and were walking side by side, Rarahu and I, along the path leading to our dwelling. A common impulse had brought us together to the homeward path, and we went on like two sulky children who do not know how to begin to make it up. We opened the door and when we were inside we looked at each other.

I expected a scene, reproaches and tears. Instead of that she smiled and looked away, with the slightest shrug of her shoulders and an unexpected look of disenchantment, of bitter melancholy and irony. This smile and shrug said as much as a very long speech; and what they said in so concise and striking a way amounted to this:

"I knew it—I knew I was only a little contemptible creature—a plaything you allowed yourself. To you white men that is all we ever can be. But what should I gain by being angry? I am alone in the world—with you or with another man, what can it signify? I have lived with you; this was our home; I know you will like to keep me with you. Well, here I am, and that is an end of it."

The simple little maid had made terrible progress in the knowledge of life; the childlike savage had outstripped her master, and could rule him. I looked at her without a word, in surprise and sadness; I felt the greatest pity for her. And it was I who asked pardon, almost with tears, as I covered her with kisses.

She, for her part, loved me still as we love some supernatural being whom we can scarcely grasp or comprehend.

Many sweet and tranquil days followed on this adventure at Afareahitu; the incident was forgotten and time went on its enervating way.

XXXV

Tiahoui, who was staying in Papeete, had come to pay us a few days' visit with two other young women of Papéuriri.

One evening she led me apart with the air of gravity which heralds a solemn interview, and we went to sit together in the garden, under the oleanders. Tiahoui was a very steady little woman, more serious than Tahitian girls commonly are. In her out-of-the-way district she had reverently imbibed all the missionary's teaching, and had the fervent faith of a neophyte. She could read Rarahu's heart like an open book, and she had discerned strange things there.

"Loti," said she, "Rarahu is being ruined at Papeete. When you are gone what is she to do?"

Rarahu's future fate was indeed a weight on my heart. Our natures were so different that I could only imperfectly apprehend all her self-contradictions and inconsistencies. And yet I understood that she was ruined, body and soul; nay, and this perhaps lent her an added charm—the charm of one doomed to die—I felt that I loved her more than ever.

Meanwhile nothing could be more gentle and more peaceful than my little Rarahu; she never fell into her old childish rages; she was almost always silent, calm and submissive. She was gracious and attentive to every one. Anyone coming to the house and seing her sitting in the shade of the verandah in a happy, careless attitude, smiling on all with the mystic smile of her race, would have said that our little hut and tall trees were the abode of a perfect poem of peaceful and entire happiness.

Then she had hours of passionate tenderness for me; it seemed as though she craved to cling to her only friend and mainstay in the world. At such moments the thought of my departure made her shed many silent tears; and then again I would recur to the insane notion of remaining here, with her forever.

At other times she would bring out the old Bible she had carried from Apiré; she would pray ecstatically, and a simple fervent faith shone in her eyes.

But then she very often withdrew from my society

and I could see on her lips the same doubtful and distrustful smile which I had first noticed that evening of our return from Afareahitu. She seemed to gaze far way and see mysterious things in the distance; strange ideas came back to her from her savage childhood, and her sudden questions about the strangest and deepest subjects showed the disorder of her imagination and the chaotic confusion of her ideas. Her Maori blood burned in her veins; she had days of fever and utter prostration when she hardly semed to be the same creature. Poor little thing, she was hardly responsible for the aberrations of her strangely ardent and vehement nature.

In appearance she had as yet none of the symptoms which, in Europe, betray disease of the lungs. Her figure was as full and as perfect as a Greek statue. But the characteristic short cough, just like that of the queen's children, became more frequent, and the blue circle round her eyes grew darker.

She was in fact a sad and pathetic personification of the Polynesian race as it gradually dies out under contact with our civilization and our vices, soon to be no more than a memory in the history of Oceania.

XXXVI

Meanwhile the hour of departure drew near; the *Reindeer* was to sail for California, "*i te fenua California*," as the queen's little granddaughter said. It was not farewell for good, indeed; on our return voyage we were to put in once more and stay in the " delicious island " for a month or two, on our way home. But for this certainty of returning, at that moment I probably should not have gone away. To leave her for ever would have been more than I could bear; it would have broken my heart.

As my departure drew near I was strangely haunted by the thought of Taïmaha, who had been my brother Rouéri's Tahitian wife. It was curiously painful to me, I know not why, to leave without having seen her, and I confessed as much to the queen, beseeching her to contrive a meeting.

Pomaré seemed to take great interest in my request.

"What, Loti," said she, "you are anxious to see her? Rouéri spoke of her then to you? He had not forgotten her?"

And the old queen sat dreaming over memories of the past, finding perhaps that she remembered some who had forgotten, some whom she had loved, and who had departed never to return.

XXXVII

It was the last evening of our stay.

The queen's hasty enquiries led to the discovery that Taïmaha had come to Tahiti only the day before, and the chief of the palace *mutoï* was instructed to convey her an order to be on the seashore, just opposite the ship, at sundown.

At the appointed hour we were on the spot, Rarahu and I. We waited a long time, and Taïmaha did not come;—I had known she would not. It was with a strange tightness about my heart that I marked the flight of these last minutes of our last evening. I waited for her with inexplicable anxiety, and I would have given a great deal at that moment to see this woman of whom I had dreamed as a boy, and who was linked in my mind with the remote and romantic memory of my brother Rouéri. And I had a presentiment that she would fail to appear.

We asked about her of some old women who went by. " She is in the high street," said they; " take our little girl with you; she knows her and will point her out. When you have found her you can send the little girl home."

XXXVIII

IN THE HIGH STREET

The noisy high street had a row of Chinese stalls on each side of it; salesmen with little almond-shaped eyes and long pig-tails were selling tea, fruits and cakes. Under all their verandahs were heaps of crowns of flowers, crowns of pandanus and *tiarés* scenting the air; the Tahitian women were wandering about singing; numbers of little lanterns, in the Chinese fashion, lighted up the booths or hung from the leafy boughs. It was one of the holiday evenings of Papeete; everything was gay and, above all, unique. The air was heavy with queer Chinese odours—sandal-wood and monoï, and the rich fragrance of gardenia and orange-flower.

It was growing late; we had not found her. Little Téhamana, our guide, looked in vain at every

face; she did not recognize one. The very name
of Taïmaha was unknown to those of whom we
made enquiry; we went to and fro among all the
groups, who stared at us as if we were out of our
wits. I was running my head against the impossi-
bility of discovering a myth, and every minute as
it passed added to my impatience and distress.

After an hour of this wandering about, in a dark
corner under some great, gloomy mango-trees,
little Téhamana suddenly stopped in front of a
woman sitting on the ground with her head in her
hands, asleep as it seemed.

"Téra!" she exclaimed. (Here she is!)

I went up to her and leaning over her, curious to
see her, I said: "Are you Taïmaha?" trembling
lest she should answer "No."

"Yes!" said she without moving.

"You are Taïmaha, wife of Rouéri?"

"Yes," she repeated, indolently raising her head.
"I am Taïmaha, wife of Rouéri the sailor, whose
eyes are asleep," (*mata moé*)—meaning "who is
dead."

"And I am Loti, Rouéri's brother.—Come away
to some quieter spot where we can talk together."

"You—his brother?" she said simply, with some
surprise but such utter indifference that I was quite
abashed. And I already repented of having stirred
these ashes to find nothing beneath but disillusion
and want of feeling.

However, she rose to follow me. I gave a hand
to each, Taïmaha and Rarahu, and went away, out
of the Tahitian throng, where no one had any
further interest for me.

XXXIX

REVELATIONS

In a deserted walk, where we could still hear the murmur of the crowd, under the black shade of the trees in the dark night, Taïmaha stopped and sat down.

"I am tired," she said to Rarahu, very wearily. "Tell him to talk to me here; I will go no further. Is he his brother?"

At this instant, an idea that had never occurred to me before flashed through my mind.

"Had you and Rouéri any children?" I asked.

"Yes," she replied, after a moment's hesitation, to me before flashed through my mind.

There was a long silence after this unexpected revelation. A tide of mixed feeling was stirred within me, feelings hitherto unknown, sad and not to be put into words. There are such situations; too startling and strange to find expression in language. The charm of a scene, the mysterious influences of nature give acuteness to our emotions or cast a glamour over them, and it becomes impossible to utter them, even ever so imperfectly.

XL

An hour later Taïmaha and I went off together, leaving Papeete asleep. This, my last evening, was at an end.

I was a prey to my strong new emotions, and for the moment had forgotten Rarahu. She had gone home alone to sit waiting and weeping in our dear little hut, where I ought to have been with her for the last time.

We walked on side by side, Taïmaha and I, swiftly making our way along the ocean strand. It had begun to rain, the warm rain of the tropics; Taïmaha, silent and thoughtful, let her long train of white muslin trail behind her, all draggled in the sand.

In the midnight calm not a sound was to be heard but the monotonous roar of the surf beating on the coral barrier, far from land. Over our heads tall palms bowed and waved; on the horizon the hill-tops of Moorea were dimly visible, rising from the blue level of the Pacific, in the doubtful light of a shrouded moon.

I looked at Taïmaha and admired her; in spite of her thirty years she was still a splendid type of Maori beauty. Her black hair fell unconfined on her white dress, and her crown of roses and pandanus-leaves gave her by night the aspect of a queen or a goddess.

I had led her on purpose past a certain old cabin half-buried in greenery and climbing plants—the hut in which she must have dwelt with my brother.

"Do you know this place, Taïmaha?" I asked her.

"Yes," said she, for the first time showing a little animation. "It was his hut, Rouéri's."

XLI

We were making our way, at this hour of the night, to the district of Faaa, where Taïmaha was to show me her youngest child, Atario. It was with a sort of condescending irony that she had lent herself to gratify this whim of mine—a fancy which to her Tahitian notions seemed almost unaccountable. In this land, where want is unknown, where there is room for every living soul in the sun and in the shade and in the water, and food for all in the woods, children grow up as the plants do, free and uncared for, wherever their parents may have chosen to place them. The family has none of the cohesion which, in Europe, it derives from the struggle for life if from no other motive.

Atario, the child born since Rouéri's departure, was living in the district of Faaa; in accordance with general practice of adoption he had been entrusted to the care of some distant relations of his mother's. And Tamaari, the elder, who had, she said, Rouéri's brow and large eyes, lived with Taïmaha's old mother in the island of Moorea which loomed out yonder, breaking the horizon with its distant peaks.

Half-way on our road we saw the glare of a fire in a coco-grove. Taïmaha took me by the hand and led me towards it by a path known to herself among the trees. When we had gone on some few minutes in the gloom, under the vault of tall palms dripping with rain, we found a thatched shelter where two old women were squatting by a fire of brushwood. Taïmaha spoke a few words which I did not understand, and the two old crones stood up to see me better; and Taïmaha, picking up a flaming brand, held it near my face and proceeded to scrutinize me with extreme attention. Not till then had we seen each other in the full light.

When her examination was ended she smiled sadly. She had no doubt traced Rouéri's familiar features in mine—the likeness between brothers is very striking to strangers, even when it is really but vague and imperfect. I, for my part, admired her fine eyes, her regular profile, and her brilliant teeth, which looked all the whiter by contrast with her coppery complexion.

Then we went on our way in silence, and presently came in sight of the huts of a district-hamlet scattered among black masses of trees.

"Tera Faaa!" (here is Faaa!) she said with a smile.

Taïmaha led me to the door of a cabin built of bourao timber, hidden away under bread-fruit trees, mangoes and tamarisk. Within, everyone seemed to be sound asleep, and she called softly through the chinks in the wall to get some one to let her in. A lamp was lighted and an old man, with only a loin-cloth on, made his appearance at the door and signed to us to come in.

The cabin was a large one; it was a sort of dormitory where several old people were sleeping. The native lamp, a wick in coco-nut oil, threw a feeble gleam of light, hardly showing the presence of all these human creatures as they lay there, swept by the sea-breeze.

Taïmaha went to a mat-bed, and took up a child, which she brought to me.

" Ah no ! " she exclaimed when she saw it by the light. " I have made a mistake; this is not the child." And she laid it down again and began to search in the other beds, but without finding the one she wanted. She carried the smoking lamp about at the end of a long wand, lighting up red-skinned old women lying rigid and motionless, wrapped in dark blue *pareos* striped with white; they might have been mummies rolled in winding sheets.

A gleam of uneasiness lighted up Taïmaha's great velvety eyes. " Old Huahara," said she, " where is Atario, my son ? "

And old Huahara leaned on her skinny elbow and fixed on us her startled eyes :

" Your son is no longer with us, Taimaha," said she; " My sister, Tiatiara-honui (spider), has adopted him. She lives five hundred paces further, at the end of the coco-grove."

XLII

On we went again, through the grove and the black night.

At Tiatiara-honui's hut the same scene was repeated—the same ceremony of awaking the sleepers, like conjuring up phantoms.

A child was roused and brought to me. The poor

little brat was dropping with sleep; he was perfectly naked. I took his head in my hands and held him close to the lamp which the old " spider," Huahara's sister, was carrying. The child, dazzled by the light, shut his eyes.

" Yes, that is Atario," said Taïmaha, who had remained by the door.

" And is that my brother's child? " I asked her in a way which ought to have gone to her heart.

" Yes," she answered, as if she understood that the question was a solemn one : " Yes, he is the son of your brother Rouéri."

Old Tiatiara-honui brought a pink frock to dress him, but the little one had fallen asleep again in my arms. I kissed him gently and laid him down again on his mat. Then I signed to Taïmaha to follow me and we took the path back to Papeete.

All this had happened as in a dream. I had scarcely had time to look at the child and yet his features remained stamped on my memory, just as at night a very clear image which we have seen but for an instant recurs and reappears again after we have shut our eyes. I was strangely upset, and my ideas were in utter confusion. I had lost all sense of time and had no notion of what hour it might be. I was in dread of seeing daybreak, and of arriving only just in time to join the *Reindeer* without being able to go back to my dear little home, or even giving a last embrace to Rarahu, whom I might never see again.

XLIII

When we were out in the air again Taïmaha asked me:

"You will come again to-morrow?"

"No," said I, "we sail quite early in the day for California."

A minute after she asked me shyly: "Rouéri had told you about Taïmaha?"

By degrees Taïmaha grew more animated as she talked; her spirit seemed to wake from a long slumber. She was no longer the same silent and indifferent creature; she questioned me in a voice full of feeling about him whom she called Rouéri and at last showed herself, as I had hoped to find her, cherishing my brother's memory with great love and deep regrets. She remembered the minutest details relating to my home and country, which she had learned from Rouéri; she still recollected even the pet name by which I had long ago been known round the dear family hearth, and smiled as she told me, reminding me at the same time of a forgotten story of my earliest childhood. I cannot describe the effect produced upon me by that name and those reminiscences, treasured in this woman's memory and repeated here in that Polynesian tongue.

The sky had cleared; as we went home it was a glorious night, and the Tahitian landscape, in the bright moonlight and the solemn silence of two in the morning, was steeped in enchantment and mystery.

I escorted Taïmaha to the door of the hut she was inhabiting at Papeete. Her usual home was with her old mother Hapoto, in the district of Téaroa in the island of Moorea. As we parted I spoke of the probable date of my return, and made her promise that she would then be at Papeete with both her boys. Taïmaha swore that she would be there; but when I mentioned her children she became gloomy and mysterious again; her last words were incoherent or mocking, her heart had closed again; as I bid her farewell I saw her just as I found her again later, incomprehensible and wild.

XLIV

It was about three in the morning when I found myself in the still alley where Rarahu awaited me. The dewy freshness of morning was in the air. Rarahu, who had remained sitting in the dark, threw her arms round my neck when I went in.

I told her of the strange adventures of the night, begging her to keep these confidences to herself, that the long forgotten tale should not now once more become the talk of all the women of Papeete.

It was our last meeting, and the uncertainty of my return, and the enormous distance that must ere long divide us, cast over all a shroud of unutterable melancholy. At this hour of parting Rarahu showed in the sweetest and tenderest light; she was altogether the little wife, and truly pathetic in her transports of love and tears. All that the purest and most heart-broken affection, the most boundless devotion can suggest to the heart of a passionate little creature, of fifteen, she poured forth in her Maori tongue, with wild extravagance and the strangest imagery.

XLV

The first pale streaks of light roused me after a few minutes' sleep. In the confusion and inexplicable distress of mind peculiar to first waking I found a medley of ideas: my departure—quitting the delicious island, abandoning for ever the hut under the tall palms and my sweet little savage love;—then Taïmaha and her children—new figures in the drama, of whom I had scarce had a glimpse during the night and who had appeared at the last moment to bind me with new ties to this distant land.

The melancholy gleam of dawn came in at the open windows. For a moment I looked at Rarahu where she slept, and then I woke her with a kiss.

"Ah, yes, Loti!" said she. "It is the day, you have woke me—we must be off. . . ."

Rarahu dressed with many tears; she put on her best tunic and crowned her head with the faded wreath and the *tiaré* she had worn yesterday, vowing that she would wear no others till my return. Then I opened the door to the garden; I cast a farewell glance at our trees and thicket of flowers. I pulled a branch of acacia, and a trailing clump of pink periwinkle—and the cat crept after us, mewing, as it used to do when we went to the bathing-place at Apiré.

Before the sun had risen my little savage wife and I, hand in hand, sadly made our way to the strand for the last time.

There a silent but numerous throng had already collected; all the queen's women, all the damsels of Papeete, whose friends or lovers the *Reindeer* was about to snatch away, were there, seated on the ground; some were weeping, others simply watched us as we came. Rarahu sat down with the rest without shedding a tear—and the last of the ship's boats carried me on board.

At about eight in the morning the *Reindeer* weighed anchor. On the shore I saw Taïmaha. She had come down to see me off, just as she had come, twelve years before, at the age of seventeen, to see the last of Rouéri, who came back no more. She caught sight of Rarahu and sat down by her side.

It was a lovely morning, calm and soft, as they are in Oceania; there was not a breath of air; heavy clouds were gathering high up among the mountains and forming a great, dark vault beneath which the morning sun blazed down on the Tahitian shore, the green coco-palms, and the figures of the women in their white robes.

The thought of departure lent the charm of melancholy to this grand picture, so soon to be lost to sight.

XLVI

When the group of Tahitian women was no more than an indistinguishable mass, my brother's deserted home was still for a long time visible on the shore of the sea, and my eyes lingered on the speck as it vanished among the trees.

The clouds gathering about the hill-tops came down rapidly over Tahiti; they fell like a huge curtain, in which the whole island was presently wrapped. The sharp peak of the precipice of Fataoua was still to be seen through a rent in the shroud, till at last all was lost in the gloomy mass; the trade-wind rose to a gale, the sea turned green and surfy and a storm of rain began to fall. Then I went below into my dingy cabin, and flung myself down in my berth, covering myself over with a blue *pareo,* torn in many places by the thorns of the forest, which Rarahu had worn long ago in her home in Apiré. There I lay all day, lulled by the monotonous noises of the rolling ship as she laboured on, the sad reiteration of the waves which beat in irregular succession on the hollow walls of the *Reindeer.* All day—sunk in the melancholy reverie which is neither sleeping nor waking, in which pictures of Oceania were strangely mingled with the dim memories of my boyhood.

In the green twilight which came in through the thick bull's-eye that closed my port-hole, I could make out all the queer objects in my room—head-dresses of Oceanian chiefs, the abortive shapes of Maori idols, grinning gods, branches of palm, branches of coral, branches of many kinds snatched at the last hour from the trees in our garden; faded but still fragrant wreaths worn by Rarahu or Ariitéa—and that last bunch of pink periwinkle pulled at the door of our little abode.

THE RAPIDS.

XLVII

Soon after sunset I was to take the watch, so I went up the companion. The keen, open air, the breeze which lashed my face, brought me back to the realities of life and a full comprehension of our departure. The officer I was to relieve for the night-watch was John B——, my good "brother John," whose gentle and faithful regard had long been my great resource in all the woes of life.

"Two islands in sight, Harry," said he, as he reported his watch. "Out there, behind us. I need not tell you what they are; you know them."

Two dim outlines, scarcely visible clouds on the horizon—Tahiti and Moorea. John remained on deck with me till a late hour; I told him all about my last night's expedition; he only had known that I had taken a long walk, and that I had something sad and unexpected to tell him. I had long lost the habit of tears, but for the last twenty-four hours I had longed to shed them, and in the darkness no one but John saw that I wept like a child.

The sea was heavy and the wind drove us on roughly, through the black night. It was like a stern awakening, this return to the hard toil of a seafaring life after a year of enervating and delicious dreams in the island which is nearest to paradise on earth.

But those distant outlines, scarcely visible clouds on the horizon—Tahiti and Moorea!

Tahiti, where at this hour Rarahu was awake and

tearful in my desolate cabin—my dear little house, beaten by the wind and rain. And Moorea, the island which held Taamari, the child " with the brow and eyes of my brother."

This child, the eldest son of our house and who is so like my brother George—how strange, is a little savage! His name is Taamari; his home—his fatherland—will for ever be unknown to him, and my old mother will never see him. And yet the sadness of the thought is sweet to me, almost a consolation. All of George, at any rate, is not at an end, did not die with him.

I, too, who shall soon perhaps be mown down by Death in some distant land, and cast into annihilation or eternity, I, too, should be glad to live again in Tahiti, in a child which would still be myself, of my blood mingled with that of Rarahu. I felt a strange gladness in the idea of such a bond between us.

I had not thought that I loved her so much, poor little thing. I am attached to her fondly and for ever; not till now had I been aware of it. Oh, how truly I loved this Oceanian island! I have two homes—far apart, to be sure; but perhaps I may return to the one I have just left—perhaps to end my days there.

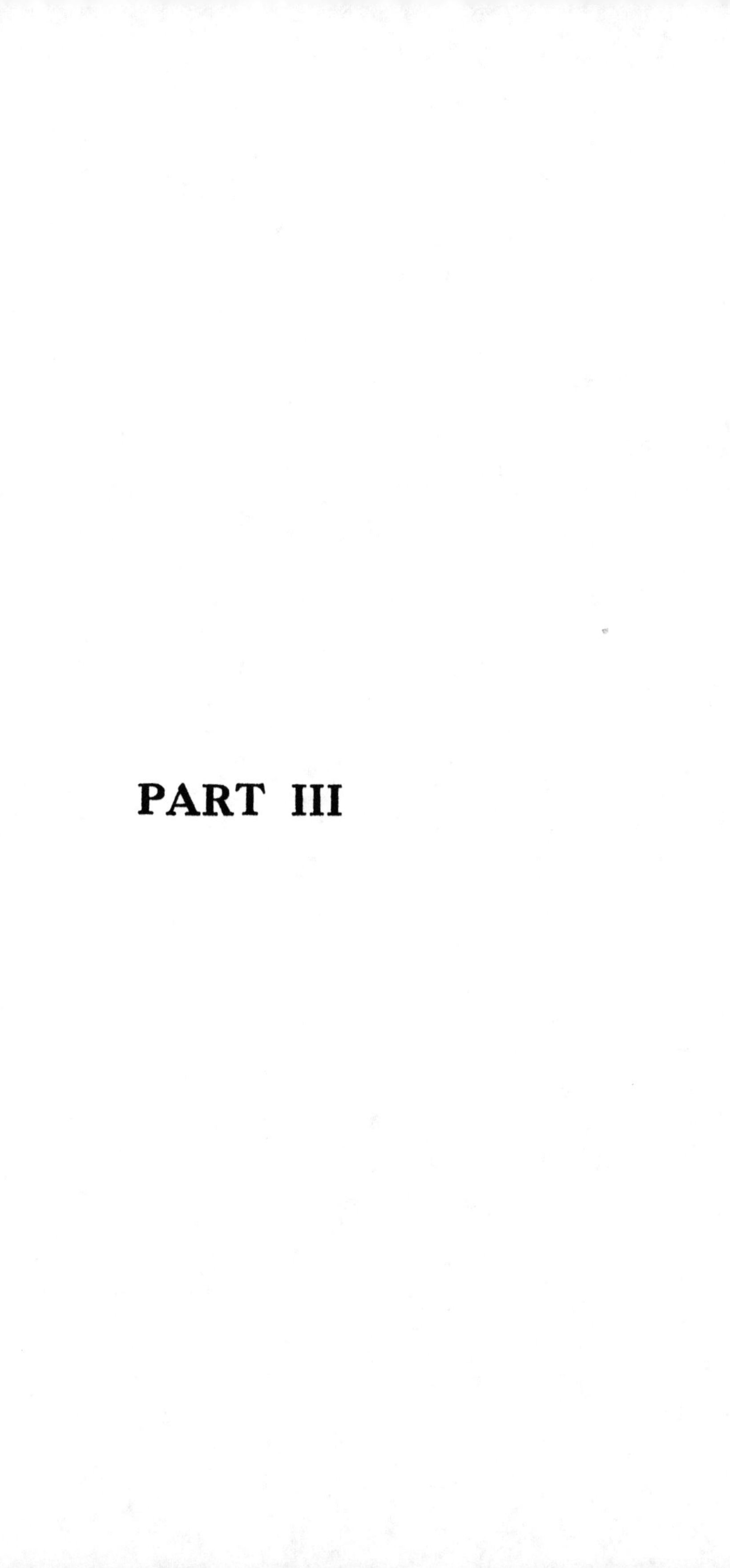

PART III

Three weeks after this the *Reindeer* put in to Honolulu, the chief town of the Sandwich Islands, where, for two months, we spent a very jolly time. Here the Maori race has already reached a stage of civilization relatively more advanced than that of Tahiti.

A very luxurious court, a gilded but leprous king, festivals in European style, ministers and generals in full uniform—and tolerably grotesque; a very droll suite altogether, forming a motley background against which the pleasing figure of Queen Emma stood out in full relief. The ladies in attendance very much dressed and bedizened; damsels of the same blood as Rarahu transformed into misses; girls just like her in type, with her rather savage look and masses of hair, but who had their many-buttoned gloves and Parisian toilets direct from France *via* Japan.

Honolulu, a large town with tramways, has a singularly mingled population; tattooed Hawaiians jostling American traders and Chinese salesmen. A beautiful land,—Nature at her best; glorious vegetation, reminding me at a distance of Tahiti, but less fresh, less lavish than that of the Isle of Ravines and of tree-ferns.

The language again is Maori; or rather a hard idiom of Maori, though of a common origin. A few words were indeed the same, and the natives could understand me. I felt less remote there from the beloved island than I did presently on the soil of America.

II

At San Francisco, in California, where we put in next, after a voyage of a month, I found lying Rarahu's first letter. It had been left with the English consul there by an American trading vessel loaded with mother-of-pearl, which had sailed from Tahiti a few days after we had left.

I te Loti—To Loti, the man who wears epaulettes, with the English admiral on board the steamship *Reindeer*.

E tau here iti e !	Oh my dear little friend !
E tau tiare noanoa no te ahiahi e !	Oh my scented evening flower !
e mea roa te mauiui no tau mafatu,	my pain is great in my heart
no te mea e aita hio au ia oe. . . .	at seeing you no more.
E tau fetia taiao e !	Oh, my star of the morning !
te oto tia nei ra tau mata	my eyes melt into tears
no te mea e aita hoi oe amuri noa tu ! . . .	because you do not return ! . . .

Ia ora na oe i te Atua mau.

> I greet you by the true God, in the Christian faith.

Na tooe hoa iti,
Rarahu.

> Your little friend
> Rarahu.

I replied in a long letter, written in correct and classic Tahitian, which a whaling vessel was to deliver by the intervention of Queen Pomaré. I assured her of my return towards the end of the year and begged her to announce it to Taïmaha and remind her of her promises.

III

THE CHINESE QUARTER—A HORS D'ŒUVRE

A grotesque reminiscence which has nothing to do with what has gone before, and still less with what is to follow; which has, indeed, no connection with my story but that of date.

The scene took place at midnight, in May, 1873, in a theatre of the Chinese quarter at San Francisco, California.

William and I, in very " scratch " undress, had gravely taken our seats in the pit. Actors, audience, scene-shifters—every one was Chinese excepting us.

We entered at the crisis of a very pathetic melodrama of which we understood not a word. The ladies in the upper circles hid their little slanting, almond-shaped eyes behind their fans, grimacing in their emotion like the figures on a china jar. The actors, dressed in the costumes of departed dynasties, gave vent to the most astonishing and incredible yells in voices for all the world like cats in a gutter; the orchestra, consisting of gongs and banjos, performed in outrageous discord—or undreamed-of harmonies.

A night scene. The lights were turned down. In front of us the long rows of shaven heads, the pit-audience, each with its preposterous decoration of a pig-tail ending in a plait of silk.

A diabolical idea took possession of us; its rapid execution was favoured by the arrangement of the benches, the darkness, and the absorbed attention of the spectators. We tied the tails together two and two and cleared out.—Oh Confucius!

IV

California, then Quadra and Vancouver, American Russia.—Six months cruising and adventures which have nothing to do with my story. In these lands we already felt ourselves nearer to Europe, and far enough from Oceania! All the Tahitian part was a dream—a dream compared with which the reality has ceased to be interesting.

In September the question was raised as to whether the *Reindeer* should not make her way home by Australia and Japan; the " white-haired admiral " was anxious to navigate the Pacific in the northern hemisphere, leaving the " delicious island " at a terrible distance to the southward. I was impotent to alter this plan which filled my soul with anguish.

Rarahu must certainly have written me several letters, but the wandering life we led, roving about the American coasts, prevented my receiving them, and I had heard nothing from her for a long time.

V

Ten months are gone by.

The *Reindeer,* which sailed from San Francisco on the 1st of November, is flying at all speed southward. For two days she has been steaming across the zone which lies between the tropics and the temperate region, and which is known as the region of semi-tropical calms.

Yesterday we were in a gloomy calm, with a grey sky overhead like that of the cooler temperate zone; the air was chilled and an unbroken curtain of motionless cloud shrouded the sun. This morning we crossed the tropic and the whole scene has suddenly changed; here is the wonderfully clear sky, the fresh breeze, warm and delicious, of the region of the trade-winds and the deep blue sea—the home of flying-fish and dolphins.

Our plans are changed; we are to return to Europe by the southern route, Cape Horn and the Atlantic. Tahiti lies in our way across the Pacific, and the admiral has decided on putting in there. It will be but for a little while, a stay of a few days, and afterwards all will be at an end for ever; but what joy to land there, especially when I had feared I should never go there again.

I was leaning over the netting gazing down into the sea. The old ship's doctor came up to me and, clapping me lightly on the shoulder, he said: " Well, Loti, I can guess what you are dreaming about. We shall soon be at your island again; indeed, we are making such good way that I think your fair Tahitian friends must be pulling us along."

" Well, doctor," said I, " if they all lent a hand, there is no knowing. . . ."

VI

November 26th, 1873.

At sea. Yesterday, under a strong gale, we made the Pomotous islands. The tropical wind is blowing hard and the sky dirty.

At noon, land—Tahiti—is in sight ahead to port. John is the first to descry it; a dim outline among the clouds: the peak of Faaa. A few minutes later the heights of Moorea are in sight to starboard, above a transparent low mist. The flying-fish rise in hundreds. The " delicious island " is there, close at hand—a strange feeling comes over me for which I have no words.

The breeze is already loaded with Tahitian perfumes, gusts of scent from orange-trees and gardenias in bloom.   A heavy pile of clouds lies over all the island.   We are beginning to distinguish greenery and coco-palms under this dark hanging. The mountain-tops glide swiftly by: Papenoo, the great bluff in Mahéna, Fataoua, then Venus-point, Fare-ute and the harbour of Papeete.

I had feared some disillusion, but the view of Papeete is enchanting.   All the golden-tinted verdure had a magical beauty in the evening sunlight.

It was about seven o'clock when we dropped anchor.   There was no one on the beach to see us arrive; by the time I set foot on shore it was dark.

The Tahitian scent which distils at night under the leaves is intoxicating; these shades are enchanted.   It is a strange joy to find myself once more in this land.

I turn down the avenue leading to the palace; it is deserted this evening.   The bourao trees have strewn it with their large, pale yellow flowers and shed leaves.   The darkness under these groves is impenetrable.   An uneasy melancholy, without any known cause, gradually comes over me in this unexpected silence; the land seems to be dead.

I walk on to Pomaré's apartments.   The queen's daughters are all there, sitting in silence.   What strange whim keeps these indolent creatures there? Formerly they would have come forth gladly to meet us.   But they are in full dress; in long white dresses with flowers in their hair—they are waiting.

One slight figure standing a little apart, more slender than the rest, attracts my eye, and I instinctively turn to her.

" Aue! Loti! " she cries, clasping me in her arms with all her might—and in the darkness I recognize the soft cheeks and fresh lips of Rarahu.

VII

Rarahu and I spent the evening wandering aimlessly about the avenues of Papeete, or in the queen's gardens. Sometimes we loitered down an alley, the first that came; sometimes we threw ourselves on the scented grass among the thick undergrowth of shrubs. They were hours of transient intoxication which we never forget as long as we live—an intoxication of the heart and senses, spell-bound by the indefinable charm and strange influencs of Oceania. And in spite of everything we were sad in the midst of our happiness at meeting again; we both felt that this was indeed the end, that very soon we must part for ever.

Rarahu had altered; in the darkness I could feel that she was more frail, and the terrible little cough was more frequent. Next day I saw that her face was paler, and pinched; she was now nearly sixteen; she was still delightfully young and childlike; but she had acquired more than ever of the mysterious stamp which in Europe we call distinction. There was really exquisite and perfect distinction in her little savage physiognomy. Her face seemed to have gained the ultra-terrestrial charm of those doomed to die.

By some extraordinary freak she had got herself placed on the staff of attendants in the palace; she had begged to be allowed to wait on Ariitéa, in whose service she was at present, and who had become very fond of her. Amid these surroudings she had imbibed some notions of the life of European women; she had begun to learn English, for my especial benefit, and she could almost speak it, with a strange little accent, indeed, very childlike and sweet. Her voice seemed softer than ever in these unfamiliar words and harsh syllables which she could not pronounce. The tongue of old England had a whimsical effect on Rarahu's lips. I listened in amazement, she seemed another woman.

Hand in hand, as of old, we made our way to the high street, which used formerly to be so full of bustle and animation. But this evening there was no singing; no young women were there, no garlands displayed under the verandahs. Even there everything was desolate. Some indefinable breath of melancholy had blown over Tahiti since our departure.

A reception was being held at the house of the French governor; we went towards the place. Through the open windows we could see into the lighted rooms; all my shipmates from the *Reindeer* were there, and all the women of the court : Queen Pomaré, Queen Moé, and Princess Ariitéa. Now and again, no doubt someone enquired : " Where is Harry Grant? " And Ariitéa would say with her dreamy smile : " He is, of course, with Rarahu, who plays at being my waiting-woman, and who was watching for him in the queen's garden before sunset."

In point of fact Loti was with Rarahu, and for

the time the rest of the world had no existence for
him.

A frail creature sitting on her nurse's knees in the
quietest corner of the room was the only person
who had seen and recognized me; her baby voice,
so weak and thin, exclaimed: " Ia ora na, Loti ! "
It was little Princess Pomaré V., the old queen's
much-loved grandchild.   I kissed her tiny hand
which she held out to me through the window, and
the incident passed unperceived by the company.

Then we wandered on again: we had no home
to which we could go. Rarahu, like me, was affected
by the sadness of everything, the silence and the
night. At midnight she had to go back to the palace
to wait on the queen and Ariitéa. We noiselessly
opened the garden gate, and went forward
cautiously to examine the premises. It was needful
to avoid being seen by old Ariifaité, the queen's
husband, who often prowls at night about the
verandahs of his residence.

The palace stood alone in a large private plot;
the white mass was plainly visible in the pale starlight; not a sound was to be heard. In this profound
stillness Pomaré's palace assumed the aspect it had
worn long ago in the dreams of my infancy. All
was sleeping; Rarahu, reassured, went up the broad
steps bidding me good-night.

I went down to the strand to find my boat and
return on board; the whole country seemed to me
overpoweringly sad that night. And yet it was a
fine Tahitian night, and the southern stars were
glorious.

VIII

Next day Rarahu quitted the service of Ariitéa, who made no difficulties. Our hut under the coco-palms, which had remained empty during my absence, was opened to receive us once more. The garden was a denser wilderness than ever, over-grown with wild shrubs and guava-trees; the pink periwinkle had spread and was blooming even in the bedroom. It was with subdued joy that we took possession of our old home. Rarahu brought back her faithful cat, who had remained her devoted friend and now made itself at home again.

And everything was like old times once more.

IX

The birds the little princess had commanded me to bring had given me infinite trouble during the voyage—the greatest trouble that birds could possibly give. About twenty survived out of thirty I had taken on board, and these, even, were much exhausted by the passage—a score of dishevelled little beings, sticky and miserable, which had been finches, linnets and goldfinches. However, the sick child accepted them gladly, and her large black eyes gleamed at the sight of them with eager delight—" That is good, very good, Loti ! " said she.

The birds had not lost one of their chief charms; featherless and ailing, they still sang, and the little queen listened to them with rapture.

X

PAPEETE, November 28th, 1873.

At seven in the morning—the most delightful hour of the day in the lands of the sun—I was awaiting Taïmaha in the queen's garden, having appointed her to meet me there.

Even in Rarahu's opinion Taïmaha was an incomprehensible creature, whom she had scarcely seen at all since my departure, and who had never chosen to give any but vague and incoherent answers on the subject of Rouéri's children.

At the hour agreed on Taïmaha made her appearance, smiling, and sat down by my side. I saw her for the first time in broad daylight—the woman who a year since had suddenly come into my ken in a half-ghostly fashion, at night, and just as I was going away.

"Here am I, Loti," said she, anticipating my first enquiries, "but my son Taamari is not with me. Twice I have asked the chief of the district to bring him; but he is afraid of the sea and refused to come. Atario, too, is no longer in Tahiti. Old Huahara sent him away to the island of Raiatéa, where one of her sisters wished for a boy."

I was fighting with the impossible—the inertia and inexplicable eccentricities of the Maori nature.

And still Taïmaha was smiling. I felt that no reproach, no entreaty would move her; I knew that neither prayers nor threats, nor even the queen's intervention would enable me to have the child I longed to see brought from so far in so short a time. And I could not bear to go away for ever without having seen him.

"Taïmaha," said I, after a moment's silent reflection, "we will go together to the island of Moorea. You cannot refuse to accompany Rouéri's brother on a voyage to see your old mother, or to show him your son."

But at the same time I sorely grudged the last few days I was to spend at Papeete and felt very jealous of these remaining hours of love and strange happiness.

XI

November 29th.

Once more the rapid chant, the noise and frenzy of the *upa-upa;* once more the crowd of Tahitian girls in front of Pomaré's palace; a last high festival in the starlight as of old.

Sitting under the queen's verandah I held Rarahu's thin hand in mine; her hair was dressed with an unwonted profusion of flowers and leaves. Close by us sat Taïmaha, telling us of her life in former years, her life with Rouéri. She had her hours of remembrance and tender emotion; she had shed real tears on recognizing a certain blue *pareo* —a poor relic of the past, which my brother had brought home long ago and which I had liked to bring back with me to Oceania.

Our expedition to Moorea was a settled thing;

only certain practical difficulties postponed its execution.

XII

December 1st, 1873.

Our start for Moorea was finally arranged very early in the morning, on the seashore. Tatari, a chief who was returning to his island, gave Taïmaha and me a passage, on the queen's recommendation. He also had with him two young men of his district, and two little girls, each leading a cat by a string. It was just opposite Rouéri's hut that we were to embark; mere chance had led to this coincidence. I had had the greatest difficulty in making a plan for this voyage; the admiral did not understand what fresh fancy took me scampering about the island of Moorea; and, in view of the short time the *Reindeer* was to remain at Papeete, for two days he absolutely refused to give me leave of absence. Moreover the prevailing winds made communications difficult between the two islands, and the date of my return to Tahiti was doubtful.

Tatari's bark was being shoved off; the pasengers had put their light baggage on board and took a cheerful leave of their friends. We were just ready. And at the last minute, Taïmaha, suddenly changing her mind, refused to go with me; she leaned her head against the wall of Rouéri's hut, and, hiding her face in her hands, she began to cry.

Neither my entreaties nor Tatari's admonitions

had the slightest effect on the woman's unexpected determination, and there was nothing for it but to go without her.

XIII

The passage took almost four hours; out at sea the wind was high and the water rough; the boat was half-full.

The two cats, tired of yelling, lay down, dripping wet, by the side of the two girls, who gave no sign of life. Thoroughly drenched, we came on land far enough from the point we aimed at, in a bay near Papetoaï—a wild and lovely spot, where we pulled the boat up high and dry on the coral. It was a long way hence to the district of Mataveri, where Taïmaha's relations lived, and with them, my brother's child. The chief sent his son Tatari with me to be my guide, and we set out along a hardly-distinguishable path under the lordly vault of palms and pandanus. Here and there we came on a hamlet built in the heart of the forest, where the natives sat in the shade as motionless and dreamy as ever, gazing at us as we went by. Young girls would come forward to greet us, laughing as they offered us opened coco-nuts and fresh water.

About half-way, we stopped at the hut of Taïrapa, the old chief of Téharoa. He was a grave, white-haired old man, who came out to meet us leaning on the shoulder of a most charmingly pretty grand-daughter.

He had in past years been in Europe and had seen the court of Louis Philippe. He told us of his impressions and amazements; I could have fancied him old Chactas relating to the Natchez Indians his visit to the " Roi-Soleil."

XIV

At about three in the afternoon I took leave of Taïrapa and went on my way. We still walked on for about an hour, along sandy paths, across lands which Tatari told me belonged to Queen Pomaré. Then we reached a lovely bay, where thousands of coco-palms rocked their heads in the gale. Under these grand trees man feels himself as insignificant, as infinitely small, as a microscopic insect creeping about among tall reeds. All these high, slender stems, were, like the soil itself, of a uniform ashen-grey; here and there a pandanus, or an oleander loaded with flowers, broke the endless colonnade with a blaze of bright colour. The bare earth was strewn with fragments of madrepores and dried palm leaves. The sea, deeply blue, broke on a strand of dead coral as white as snow; on the horizon Tahiti was in sight, half-hidden in mist, basking in the broad tropical sunshine. The wind whistled mournfully under the palms, as if they were enormous organ-pipes; my head was full of gloomy thoughts and strange impressions—and the memory of my brother, which I had come hither to find, revived like the visions of my childhood, in the night of the past.

XV

" Here," said Tatari, " are the various members of Taïmaha's family; the child you are in search of will be here, and its old grandmother, Hapoto."

Before us, in fact, a group of natives were sitting in the shade; women and children, whose dusky forms were seen against the sparkling sea beyond. My heart beat high as I went towards them at the thought that I was about to see the unknown child, already loved, the poor little savage, bound to me by the closest ties of blood.

" This is Loti, Rouéri's brother; this woman is Hapoto, Taïmaha's mother," said Tatari, showing me an old woman who held out a tattooed hand. " And here is Taamari," he added, pointing to a child sitting at my feet.

I embraced this child of my brother with an impulse of affection. I looked at him, trying to recognize the long-dead features of Rouéri. He was a sweet little fellow, but in his round face I could see only a likeness to his mother; he had the black velvety eyes of Taïmaha.   It struck me, too, that he was very young; in this land, where men and plants grow up quickly, I had looked for a great boy of thirteen, with an expression of depth, like George's; and for the first time a bitter, cruel doubt flashed across my mind.

XVI

It was no easy matter to verify the date of Taamari's birth; I questioned the woman in vain. In a land where the seasons pass unmarked in a perpetual summer, the idea of dates is imperfect; years are scarcely counted.

"However," said Hapoto, "certain writings, something like a register of the births of all the children of the family, were deposited with the chief, and they were preserved in the *farehau* of the district."

At my request a young girl went off to fetch them from the village of Tehapeu, saying it would take her two hours to go and return.

The spot where I now found myself was both grand and terrible; nothing in Europe can give the faintest notion of these Polynesian landscapes. Such splendour and such melancholy were created to feed other imaginations than ours. Behind us tall peaks pierced the clear, deep upper air. All round the bay, which stretched in a vast circle, the palms were waving their tall heads. The vivid tropical light blazed over all. The wind from the sea blew a gale; dead leaves whirled along in eddies; the sea on the coral made a great noise.

I looked at the group about me. It struck me that they differed from the people of Tahiti; their grave faces had a more savage look.

By dint of much voyaging the mind grows torpid; we become accustomed to everything and anything —to the strangest exotic scenery and the most extraordinary physiognomies. At certain times, however, when the spirit is roused and recovers itself, it is suddenly startled by the singularity of the surroundings.

I looked on these natives as strangers—deeply conscious for the first time of the radical difference of our races, our ideas and our way of seeing things. Though I was dressed like them and understood their speech, I was as much alone in their midst as in the barest desert island. The awful distance which lay between me and the speck of land I call home weighed on my soul—the vastness of the sea— my own utter solitude.   Then I looked at Taamari and called him to me; he leaned his little brown head against my knees, quite tame. And my thoughts flew off to my brother George, sleeping to all eternity in the depths of the ocean, far away, by the coast of Bengal.—This child was his son—and a family descended from us would survive in these lost islands.

" Loti," said old Hapoto, rising, " come and rest in my hut, which is on the opposite shore, about five hundred paces further on. There you can eat and sleep; you will find my son there and can settle with him as to how to get back to Tahiti with this child whom you wish to take."

XVII

Old Hapoto's cabin was but a few yards from the shore. It was the regular Maori structure, with the old paving of black flags, the lattice walls, and the pandanus thatch—a haven for scorpions and centipedes. Massive beams of timber supported large beds of an old-fashioned pattern, with curtains made of the macerated and flattened bark of the paper-mulberry. A clumsy table, with these primitive bedsteads, formed the whole of the furniture; but on the table lay a Bible in Tahitian, reminding the visitor that the Christian religion was held in honour in this remote dwelling.

Téharo, Taïmaha's brother, was a man of five-and-twenty, with a gentle, intelligent countenance; he retained a lively memory of my brother, a mixture of respect and affection, and he welcomed me with joy. He had at his command the boat belonging to the chief of the district, and we agreed to start for Tahiti as soon as the wind and the waves would allow.

I told him that I was accustomed to native food, and should be content like the rest of the family with bread-fruit. But Hapoto had ordered great preparations to be made for my evening meal, which was to be a banquet. Several fowls were pursued and done to death, and a great fire was made on the ground to cook the *feii* for me, and the bread-fruit.

XVIII

Meanwhile time went but slowly. It would still
be an hour before the girl who had gone to seek the
certificates of birth of Taïmaha's children, could
return. While I waited I took a walk along the seashore with my new friends—a walk which has left
on my mind an impression as weird as a dream.

From the spot where we were, as far as Afareahitu, whither we were walking, the country is no
more than a narrow strip of land winding along the
shore, between the sea and the peaked bluffs, to
whose sides impenetrable forests cling. Around me
everything seemed more gloomy each moment. The
evening, the loneliness, the uneasy fears which per-
vaded my being, gave a desolate tone to the landscape.

Coco-palms and yet more coco-palms, with
oleanders and pandanus—all strangely tall and
slender and bowed by the wind. The long palm-
trunks swaying in all directions were occasionally
hung with streamers of lichen like long grey hair.
And under our feet the bare grey soil, pierced in
every direction by crabs.

The way we went seemed utterly deserted; the
blue land crabs had taken possession; they scrambled
away before our feet with the queer noise they make
at nightfall.   The mountain was already dipped in
shadow.

Téharo walked by my side, a tall figure, thoughtful

and silent as Maoris are; I led my brother's child by the hand.

Now and again Taamari's sweet voice rose up among the solemn, monotonous sounds of nature; his childish questions were singular and incoherent. But I had no difficulty in understanding the little fellow, whom many of those who speak the " 'long shore " dialect would have failed to follow, for he spoke the old Tahitian tongue, almost in its purity.

We presently saw in the distance a canoe under sail, very rashly returning from Tahiti; however, it presently got in, under the lee of the barrier reef, almost on its beam ends under the heavy trade-wind. Some natives sprang out, and two young girls, who ran off, dripping wet, casting the startling sound of laughter to the melancholy breeze. And an old Chinaman got out, in a black gown, and he stopped to caress little Taamari and took some cakes out of his bag to give him.

The old man's notice of the boy and his look suggested a horrible fear.

The day was drawing to a close, the palm-trees were wrung overhead, shaking down on us their population of scorpions and centipedes. Gusts came tearing past, bending the trees like a field of reeds, and dead leaves danced wildly along the ground. I reflected, very naturally, that I should probably have to stay here some days before a canoe could possibly put out to sea. This is of frequent occurrence between Tahiti and Moorea.

The *Reindeer* was to sail early in the following week. My absence would not delay her a single hour—and the last moments I might have spent with Rarahu—the last in all my life—would thus have fled, far from her side.

By the time we returned it was quite dark. I had not thought of this night, nor foreseen the sinister impression I felt at its approach. I was beginning, too, to feel the dulness of limb and burning thirst of fever, brought on, no doubt, by the acute experiences of the day, added to excessive fatigue.

We sat down outside old Hapoto's hut. There were several girls there, crowned with flowers, who had come forth from the huts in the neighbourhood to see the *paoupa*—stranger—for rarely is one seen in the district.

" Why ! " said one of them coming up to me—" Is it you, Mata-reva?"

It was long indeed since I had heard that name; which Rarahu had given me long ago, but which had been superseded by that of Loti. This damsel had learnt it at Apiré, by the brook Fataoua, where she had seen me the year before.

Under the influence of fever and of the night, nature and all things assumed strange and unaccustomed aspects. In the woods on the mountain-side the plaintive monotonous call of the reed-pipes could be heard.

A few yards away, under a thatched roof raised on poles of bourao-wood, a grand cooking was going on for my benefit. The wind swept terribly through this kitchen; naked men, with great heads of towzled hair, were squatting there round a dense wreath of smoke; and the word *Toupapahou* sounded weirdly close to my ears.

XIX

Before this, the girl who had been sent to the chief of the district had returned; I had read the few lines of Tahitian which verified the dates, by the last glimmer of daylight:

Taamari, born of Taïmaha, the fifth day of July, 1864.
Atario, born of Taïmaha, the second day of August, 1865.

My heart sank—collapsed, as though a void had formed there; I would not see; I would not believe. It was strange, but I had clung to the idea of this Tahitian family, and the emptiness within gave me mysterious and acute pain; it seemed as though my lost brother were now cast more utterly and for ever into annihilation; all that might have been left him was sunk in deepest night; it was as if he had died a second time.—And the islands on a sudden were desolate, all the witchery of Oceania was killed at one blow, nothing bound me any longer to this land.

"Are you quite sure, Loti," said Taïmaha's mother in a quavering voice—poor old half-savage creature—"Are you quite sure of what you say?"

And I solemnly assured them that it was all a lie. Taïmaha had done what so many of those incomprehensible Tahitian women do; after Rouéri's departure she had taken up another European lover.

There is very little communication between the district of Matavéri and Papeete; she had been able to cheat her mother, her brother, and her sisters, by concealing from them for two years the departure of the man to whom they had given her; and then she had come back, bewailing him, to Moorea. And she had really mourned for him; perhaps indeed he was the only man she had loved.

Little Taamari still sat by me, his head leaning against my knees. Old Hapoto pulled him away roughly by the arm. Then she hid her face in her wrinkled and tattooed hands, and a minute after I heard her sob.

XX

Then I sat a long time, holding the papers sent by the chief, and trying to sort my ideas, all confused by fever. I had allowed myself to be cheated like a silly child by the mere word of this woman; I cursed the creature who had brought me to this desolate island, while Rarahu was awaiting me in Tahiti, and irretrievable time was flying from both of us.

The girls sat there still, with their wreaths of gardenia perfuming the evening; they were all motionless, their heads turned towards the forest, in a close group, as though in combination to oppose the growing darkness, the solitude, and the terrors of the woods.

The gale was rising, it was chill and dark.

XXI

I did small justice to the supper they had made ready for me, and Téharo having given up his bed to me, I lay down on the white matting to try for sleep to soothe my troubled brain. Téharo undertook to watch till daybreak, that nothing might delay our start for Tahiti if the wind should fall towards morning.

The family ate their evening meal, and then all stretched themselves in silence on their beds of dry leaves, rolled up like Egyptian mummies in their dark-coloured *pareos,* their heads resting in the antique fashion, on props made of bamboo.

The lamp of coco-nut oil, after flickering for a while in the wind, went out, and the darkness was complete.

XXII

Then began a strange night, full of fantastic visions and terrors. The hangings of paper-mulberry tissue fluttered about me with rustlings like bats' wings, the tremendous sea breeze swept over my head. I shivered with cold in my *pareo;* I endured all the fears, all the misery of a castaway child. How can I find, in any European tongue, words which at all represent that night in Polynesia, those heart-broken sounds of nature—of the vast sonorous words; the loneliness of the infinite Ocean; the forests, full of uncanny piping and murmurs, peopled with phantoms—the Toupapahous of Oceanian legend wandering through the wood, with doleful cries, blue faces, sharp teeth, and long dishevelled hair.

Towards midnight I heard outside a distinct sound of human voices, which brought comfort to me, and then a hand gently took mine.   It was Téharo, who had come to see whether I still was feverish.   I told him that I had moments of delirium and strange visions, and begged him to remain with me.   These things are familiar to the Maoris and never amaze them.   He held my hand between his own, and his presence brought peace to my imagination.   Presently, too, as the fever took its course, I ceased to feel so cold, and at last I fell asleep.

XXIII

At three in the morning Téharo woke me.

At that moment I was far away—at Brightbury, lying in my room as a child under the blessed roof of my old home; I thought I heard the old lime-trees under my window rubbing their moss-grown branches together, and the familiar tune of the stream under the poplars; but they were the coco-palm leaves that were rustling and creaking, and the sea sending up its eternal plaint from the coral reef.

Téharo called me to be off.   The weather had mended, and the canoe was getting ready.

When I got into the open air I felt better, but I was still feverish and my head was dizzy.   The

Maoris were going and coming on the beach in the darkness, bringing spars, sails, and paddles. Wearied out I lay down in the bottom of the boat and we were off.

XXIV

It was a moonless night; still, by the diffused starlight I saw distinctly the forests hanging overhead, and the white trunks of the tall, bending coco-palms.

The gale sent us off at a pace which was very rash for navigating the barrier reef in the depth of the night; the natives muttered their alarm in low tones at running before the wind in such weather, and in the dark. The canoe did indeed several times graze the coral. Those terrible white snags scraped its keel with a hollow noise, but they broke off, and we got through. In the open there was less wind, and suddenly a dead calm fell. Rolled on a tremendous swell, and in utter darkness, we were making no way; the men had to ply their paddles.

Meanwhile I had recovered; I could sit up and I took the steering. Then I saw that an old woman was lying at the bottom of the canoe; it was Hapoto, who had come with us to speak with Taïmaha.

By the time the sea had calmed down like the wind, it was near daybreak. We soon saw the first gleams of dawn, and the tall peaks of Moorea, already in the distance, took a faint tint of rose. The old woman lying at my side was motionless, and I thought she had fainted; but the Maoris respected her slumbers, so like death, the result of fatigue and

intense alarm; they spoke in undertones, not to
disturb her.

Each of us in turn performed his toilet by plung-
ing into the sea; after which we made cigarettes of
pandanus, while watching for the sun to rise.

The morning was calm and glorious; all the
phantoms of the night had fled. I shook off those
dismal dreams with an all-pervading sense of
physical relief. And presently, when I saw Tahiti,
Papeete, the queen's house, my brother's hut—all in
the clear early sunshine, and Moorea, no longer dark
but basking in light, I knew how well I still loved
this country, in spite of the gulf which had opened
before me and the absence of those non-existent ties
of blood—and I fairly ran down the path to the dear
little home where Rarahu was waiting for me.

XXV

The day fixed on by the little princess for freeing
her singing-birds had come.

A party of five of us were to assist at this im-
portant transaction, and a carriage of the queen's
having conveyed us to the immediate neighbourhood
of Fataoua, we went on foot into the wood.

Little Pomaré, who had been entrusted to our
care, walked gently and slowly between Rarahu and
me, each of us holding a hand; two waiting-women
followed, carrying the cage and its precious inhabitants on a stick.

In a delicious nook of the Fataoua woods, far
from every human habitation, the child stopped. It

was evening; the sun, already low, shot no ray through the thick cover of the forest and, above the vegetation, the towering bluffs cast their shadows across the land. A dim blue light falling from above, as into a cellar, showed the earth carpeted with exquisite and delicate ferns; under the taller trees lemon shrubs were white with blossom. The tumbling water-fall could be heard through the damp air; all else was silence, the silence of the Polynesian forest—a land of ominous enchantment, where life seems quite extinct.

Pomaré's little granddaughter, very serious and grave, herself opened the door of the cage, and then we all drew back so as not to scare them in their escape.

But the little creatures seemed very little disposed to take flight. The first to put its head out of the door, a fine linnet without a tail, seemed to reconnoitre the ground very attentively, and then it went in again, frightened by the silence and solemnity of the scene, no doubt saying to the others : " We shall not get on well in this country; the Creator has not put any birds here; these groves were never made for us."

We had to catch them in our hands to get them out, and when they were all at liberty, hopping from branch to branch with anxious enquiry, we left them there.

It was by this time almost dark, and the poor little things seemed to follow us, piping among the leaves. We heard them behind us till we were out of the woods.

.   .   .   .

XXVI

I cannot express the strange effect it had on me to hear Rarahu speak English. She was fully aware of this, and never used it excepting when she was very sure of what she meant to say and wished me to be greatly impressed by it. At such moments her voice had an indescribable sweetness, and a quaint, penetrating charm of sadness. Some words and phrases she pronounced very well, and then I could fancy her a daughter of my own race and blood; it seemed suddenly to bring us closer together in a mysterious and unexpected way. She saw now that it was vain to think of keeping me with her; that this notion was past and gone like a dream of childhood; that all this was quite impossible and done with for ever. Our days were numbered. At most could I talk of returning, and she had ceased to believe me. What she had done during my absence I knew not; she had taken up no other sailor lover, and this was all I asked. I had not lost a sort of prestige over her imagination; absence had not broken it, and no one else could have exerted it. On my return she had lavished on me all the love that a passionate little being of sixteen has to give;—and yet, I saw it clearly, as time flew on, day by day, Rarahu was slipping from me. She smiled with the same quiet smile, but her heart, I knew, was full of bitterness, of disenchantment, of obscure wrath, and all the seething passions of a savage child.

And I loved her all the time, God knows! It was torture to leave her and know that she was lost.

" My sweet little girl," I would say to her, " You must be very good when I am gone. God willing, I will come back to you. You, too, believe in God; then pray, at any rate pray, and we shall meet again beyond the grave."

" You must go away," I said, on my knees to her. " Go far away from this town of Papeete. Go and live with your little friend Tiahoui, in a country district, far away from any Europeans. You will marry as she has done, and have a family like a Christian woman and then with little ones belonging to you and which you will bring up yourself, you will be happy."

And then, and always, her lips wore the same inscrutable smile; she hung her head but made no reply. I knew full well that when I was gone she would be one of the wildest of the lost among the damsels of Papeete.

Good God! what misery it was when she, silent, and absent-minded, to all I could say to her of passionate entreaty only smiled that smile of mournful indifference, of doubt and irony.

Is there any suffering to compare with this—of loving and feeling you are no longer listened to? That the heart which has been yours is closing against you, do what you will? That the dark and unaccountable side of her nature is reasserting all its claims and all its power? And, all the time, to love with all your soul this soul which is slipping away from you.

And then Death lurks in the background; it must lay hands ere long on that beloved form, flesh of your flesh.   Death without resurrection or hope, since the one who is doomed to die has lost all faith in salvation and another life.

If that soul were altogether lost and reprobate it might be sacrificed as an impure thing. But to know that it is in anguish, that it has been so sweet, and loving, and pure! It is like a shroud of darkness enfolding it, a foretaste of death which chills and encloses it. It might yet be possible to save it— but we must part, part for ever; time flies, nothing can be done.

Then come transports of love and tears. At the very last before the end we fain would make the most of the bliss so soon to be snatched from us.

. . . .

XXVII

Rarahu and I were walking hand in hand along the path to Apiré. It was two days before I must sail.   The heat was oppressive and stormy; the air heavy with the scent of ripe guavas; all the plants seemed flagging. Young coco-trees with golden yellow plumes stood out against a dull leaden sky; the peak of Fataoua showed its horns and teeth among clouds; the basalt cliffs seemed literally to weigh hot and heavy on our heads and to oppress our minds as well as our senses.

Two women, who seemed to be waiting for us by the road, rose as we approached, and came to meet us. One—old, broken, and tattooed—dragged the other, who was still young and handsome, along by the hand. They were Hapoto and her daughter Taïmaha.

"Loti," said the old woman humbly, "forgive Taïmaha!"

Taïmaha was smiling her everlasting smile; her eyes cast down like a child caught in mischief, but quite unconscious of the wrong it has done, and devoid of all remorse.

"Loti," said Rarahu in English, "forgive her."

I forgave the woman and took the hand she held out to me. It is impossible for us, born on the other side of the world, to judge, or even to understand these incompletely-developed natures, so different from our own; at bottom always so mysteriously savage, and in which there is at times so much charm, and love, and exquisite feeling. Taïmaha had a very precious object to restore to me—a relic of the past—Rouéri's *pareo* which, by her request, I had entrusted to her. She had washed and mended it with the greatest care. And she was moved, too, for a tear trembled in her eye as she gave me back this remembrance which was to go back with me to Brightbury whence I had brought it.

XXVIII

In the course of my last visit to Queen Pomaré I besought her to care for Rarahu.

The old woman shook her head.

"And what then, Loti," said she. "What could you do for her?"

" I will come back," said I, not too confidently.

" Loti, your brother was to have come back!—You all say that," she went on slowly, as if recalling her own memories. " When you leave my country you all say so. But the land of Britain (te fenua piritania) is far away. Of all I have seen depart, very few have returned.—But kiss her, at any rate," she added, pointing to her granddaughter—" for you will never see her again."

XXIX

That evening Rarahu and I sat together under the verandah of our hut; on all sides the crickets in the grass were chirping their summer-evening song. The unpruned boughs of orange and hibiscus gave the spot a neglected and uncared-for appearance; we were half-hidden under their twisted and bushy growth.

" Rarahu," said I, " can you no longer believe in the god of your childhood, whom you used to love and worship? "

" When a man is dead," she slowly replied, " and buried underground, can anyone make him come out of it again? "

" And yet," said I, trying to work on some beliefs which she had not lost, " and yet you are afraid of ghosts; you know that even at this very hour, close to us, among the trees perhaps. . . ."

" Oh, yes," she cried with a shudder, " after death there is perhaps the *toupapahou;* after death there may be a ghost, which sometimes appears again and prowls about the woods. But I think that even the *toupapahou* perishes, too, at last when there is no shape left under the ground—and that is the end of everything."

I shall never forget the clear, childish voice uttering these gloomy things in that strange soft tongue.

XXX

It was the last day.

The southern sun had risen as purely bright as usual on " Delicious Tahiti." Eternal nature has no concern with what men's hearts may suffer as they come and vanish, and never lets it darken her unconscious gladness.

All day we had been on our feet and much hurried. The preparations for departure sometimes bring a happy diversion of mind to those who must part, and this was our case. We had all the treasures of our fishing-excursions on the reef to pack up; shells and rare corals, which had dried, during my absence, on the grass in our garden, and now looked like masses of the finest and most complicated lichens bleached whiter than snow.

Rarahu was extremely energetic and did a great deal of work, which is unusual with the women of Tahiti; all this bustle cheated her grief. I felt that her heart was breaking at seeing me leave. She was herself once more and I began to recover a little confidence and hope.

We had a great variety of things to stow away

—things which would have made some folks smile; some guava boughs from Apiré, some branches out of our garden, chips of bark off the tall palms which shaded our hut. Some of Rarahu's faded garlands, too, all she had worn these last few days were to be part of my baggage, with sheafs of ferns and masses of flowers. And to these Rarahu added bunches of *reva-reva* shut up in boxes of sweet-smelling wood, and frail crowns of *peïa* straw which she had had plaited for me. And all this filled huge boxes and cases, and constituted a vast amount of luggage.

XXXI

By two o'clock these great preparations were complete—Rarahu put on her best white muslin *tapa*, dressed her unbraided hair with gardenias, and we left the house.

Before leaving I wanted to see Faa once more, and its tall coco-palms and broad coral strand; to cast a parting glance at these Tahitian scenes; to see Apiré again and plunge once more in the waters of Fataoua. I had to say good-bye to a number of native friends; I wanted to see everything, everybody, I could not bear to be leaving it all.—And the hours were flying, and we could not make up our minds what to do first.

None but those whose fate it has been to quit for ever places and beings so dear to them can understand the agitations of this departure—the aching anxiety which becomes as oppressive as physical suffering.

It was getting late by the time we reached Apiré and the bathing place of Fataoua. But there, at any rate, nothing had changed since the good old time; on the banks the company was numerous and select; Tétouara the black woman still reigned supreme over her court, and a crowd of girls were swimming and diving like so many fish, as careless and as happy.

We went past the throng, hand in hand as of old, and saying good-day right and left to the many friendly faces. As we approached, the laughter ceased. Rarahu's forlorn and serious little face, her white trailing dress like a bride's, and her sad eyes had produced silence. The Tahitians are quick to understand the feelings of the heart, and respect sorrow. Rarahu was acknowledged by all as " Loti's little wife "; it was recognized that the attachment which bound us was no commonplace affair; and above all it was known to all that this was the last time we should be seen together.

We turned off to the right, along the familiar path. Only a little further up, under the dismal shade of guava-trees, was the basin which had been Rarahu's nursery, and which we had been used to regard as more or less our particular property.

We found there two girls, strangers, and very handsome in spite of the savage hardness of their features; one was dressed in rose colour, the other in pale green; their hair, as black as night, was closely wavy like that of the women of Nuka-Hiva, and they had, too, the same expression of savage irony. Seated on boulders in mid-stream, their feet dipping in the water, they were singing an air of the Marquesas isles in husky tones. They fled as we appeared, and we were left alone as we had hoped to be.

XXXII

We had not revisted this spot since the *Reindeer's* return to Tahiti. As we found ourselves once more in this nook, which had been our very own, we felt deep emotion, and at the same time a sensation of delight which no other spot on earth could possibly have caused us.

Everything was exactly as it had always been in this spot where the air was always fresh with running waters; we knew every stone, every bough—everything, down to the tiniest mosses. Nothing had changed; there were the very same growths and the same perfume, a mixture of aromatic plants and ripe guavas.

We hung our dresses on the branches, and, wrapped in our *pareos,* sat down in the water, feeling it delightful to be here once more, for the last time, at sunset, in the ripples of the Fataoua. This clear, delicious flood came down from Oroena by the great upper fall; it danced over large polished rocks, between which slender guava shrubs were rooted. The boughs arched in a vault overhead, and the myriad outlines of their leaves dappled the eddying mirror. The ripe fruit fell into the water and was carried down the stream, whose bed was strewn with guavas, oranges and lemons.

Neither of us spoke; seated side by side, we could read each other's sad thoughts, without needing to break the silence by speech. Tiny fishes and minute blue lizards came out and about, as though no human being were there; we were so still that even the timid *varos* came out from between the stones and wandered round us.

The sun, already low, the setting sun of my last evening in Oceania, cast a warm golden glow on some of the tree-tops—I admired it all for the last time. The sensitive plants were folding up their delicate leaves; the airy acacias and dark guava shrubs already wore their evening tints—and this evening was the last;—and to-morrow at daybreak I should be gone never to return. This land, and my beloved little companion, would vanish from my ken like the scenery of an ended act in the drama.

This act had been a fairy-scene in the midst of my life; but it was ended beyond remedy. The dreams, the agitations—sweet and intoxicating or keenly grievous—all was at an end, all dead.

And I looked at Rarahu, whose hand I was holding. Large tears rained down her cheeks; silent tears, which flowed fast, the overflow of a vase full to the brim.

"Loti," said she, "I am yours—I am your little wife, am I not?—Do not be afraid for me; I believe in God; I do pray—I will pray.—I will do all you ask me, everything. To-morrow when you go I will leave Papeete, and never be seen there again. I will go to live with Tiahoui; I will have no other husband, and till I die I will pray for you...."

And here sobs cut short her words, and Rarahu

put her arms round me and laid her head on my knees. I shed tears too, but they were tears of comfort; I had found my litle girl as she had been of old; she was crushed, but she was saved. I could bear to leave her now—for fate must part us inexorably and irrevocably; but the parting was less full of bitterness and heart-rending terrors. I could leave her with a doubtful but consoling hope of returning—and with perhaps a vague hope of eternity.

.　.　.　.　.　.　.　.　.　.　.　.　.　.

XXXIII

There was a grand ball at the palace that evening, a farewell entertainment to the officers of the *Reindeer*. We were to dance till it was time to get under sail, and this " the white-haired admiral " had fixed for sunrise. Rarahu and I would be there.

The ball was enormously crowded—for Papeete. All the Tahitian women about the court, a few European ladies—as many as the colony could furnish; all the officers of the *Reindeer,* and all the French governor's staff.

Rarahu, of course, was not admitted as one of the company; but while the common crowd were dancing a wild *upa-upa* in the gardens, she and a few other young women filling similar situations, by privilege of the queen had been invited to occupy a bench under the verandah, whence they could see and be seen just as well as if they had been inside. And in the free Tahitian way it was quite a matter of course that I should go at frequent intervals to the open window and chat with Rarahu. As I danced I constantly caught her solemn gaze. She was lighted up like a vision with the ruddy glare of the lamps on one side, and the blue moonbeams on the other; her white tunic and necklace of beads shone out against the darkness beyond.

Towards midnight the queen beckoned me to her; her litle sick granddaughter, who had insisted on being dressed for this ball, was being carried to bed. Little Pomaré wished to take leave of me before she went to sleep.

In spite of everything the ball was a sad function. The greater number of the guests were the ship's officers, and this cast a gloom of departure and parting which nothing could lift. There were young men among them who were leaving behind a life of careless enjoyment; and there were old men, too, old hands who had been to Tahiti two or three times in the course of their lives, and who knew that the end had come, with a chill at their heart as they reflected that they would return no more.

Princess Ariitéa came up to me, more eager than was usual with her, and speaking more quickly:

" Loti," said she, " the queen begs you will go to the piano and play the noisiest waltz you can; and play very fast, and then go on without interruption with another dance-tune—and then a third—so as to put some life into the ball which seems as if it were dying. . . ."

I played with frenzy, stunning myself even,

everything by way of music that lay on the piano. For an hour I succeeded in keeping the ball alive; but it was a mere semblance of vitality, and I could keep it up no longer.

XXXIV

At three in the morning, when the room was empty, I was still at the piano playing heaven knows what mad tunes, to the distant accompaniment of the *upa-upa* which was dying hard outside. I was alone with the old queen, who still sat pensive and motionless in her great gilt chair. She looked like some gloomy and dissipated old idol decked out in half-savage splendour.

The room had the dejected aspect of a deserted ball-room, utter disorder and emptiness, with wax-lights burning out in the candelabra and flickering in the night breeze.

The queen rose stiffly in the heavy folds of her crimson velvet dress. She caught sight of Rarahu standing near the door, and silently looking in. Pomaré understood and signed to her to come in. Rarahu obeyed, timidly, with downcast eyes, and drew near to the queen. Appearing thus after the ball was over in this deserted hall and silence, with her long train of white muslin, her bare feet, her long hair crowned with white gardenias, and her eyes looking the larger for her tears, she looked like a *willi*, an exquisite vision of the night.

" You would wish to speak to me, Loti, no doubt; you would like to ask me to watch over her," said the old queen very kindly. "But she herself, I fear, would not like that. . . ."

"Madam," said I, "she is going away to-morrow, to Papéouriri, to ask her friend Tiahoui to give her a home. There, as here, I beseech you to protect her. She will be seen no more at Papeete."

"Ah!" said the queen in her gruff voice, evidently moved, "that is well, my child, that is well. At Papeete you would soon have been ruined."

We both shed tears; nay, indeed, all three; the old queen held our hands, and her eyes, usually so stern, were moist.

"Well, then, my child," she went on, "we must not delay your departure. If it will not take you long—as I fancy—to make your arrangements, will you set off this morning soon after sunrise, at about seven o'clock, in the carriage which is to convey my daughter-in-law, Moé?—Moé is going to Atimaono to join the ship which is to take her home to Raïatéa. You will sleep to-night at Maraa, and to-morrow morning go on to Papéouriri, where the carriage will set you down on the way."

Rarahu smiled through her tears at the notion, which filled her with childish delight, of travelling with the young Queen of Raïatéa.

There was a mysterious affinity between Rarahu and Moé; both singularly unhappy and heart-broken, they had very much the same nature, with the same manner and the same kind of charm.

Rarahu replied that she would be ready. Indeed,

poor little thing, she had nothing to carry with her but a few muslin dresses of different colours, and her faithful grey cat.

So we took leave of Pomaré, pressing her royal old hands with effusive gratitude and all our hearts. Princess Ariitéa, who had come into the room again, accompanied us in her ball-dress to the garden gate, saying to Rarahu the sweetest things to comfort her, as she might have done to her sister. And for the last time we went down to the beach.

XXXV

It was still quite dark. Large knots of people had gathered on the seashore; all the girls about the court, in the dresses they had worn in the evening, had come down with the officers of the *Reindeer*. Excepting that here and there a woman might be heard to sob, it was more like a holiday than a parting.

And there, just before daybreak, I kissed my little Tahitian wife for the last time.

At the same hour in which the *Reindeer* sailed away from the " delicious isle " the carriage conveying Moé and Rarahu left Papeete—and for a long time yet, through the breaks in the coco-nut grove over screens of greenery, Rarahu could see the *Reindeer* on the immense expanse of blue.

PART IV

> "Aue ! Aue! a munaiho te
> tiaré iti tarona menehenehe! . . .
> "Aue! Aue! i teienei ra, ua
> maheahea! . . ."
> (*Alas! Alas! the little arum
> flower was once so pretty!
> Alas! Alas! now it is faded.*)
> (Rarahu.)

I

A few days later the *Reindeer,* in her course across
the Pacific sighted the hill-tops of Rapa, the most
southerly of the Polynesian islands. And then the
last spot of Maori land disappeared from our vast,
monotonous horizon—and that was an end to
Oceania. After putting into Chile, we quitted the
great ocean by the Straits of Magellan, returning to
Europe by La Plata, Brazil and the Azores.

II

On a melancholy March morning, in the doubtful
dawn of a foggy day, I was once more at Brightbury, knocking at the door of my dear old home. I
was not expected so soon. I fell into my old
mother's arms, she trembling with surprise and
emotion. Great were the joy and astonishment of
all at seeing me back again.

After the first moments a sense of sadness follows on such rejoicing; a tightness about the heart mingles with pleasure of being at home once more; years have elapsed since the last parting—we look at those dear to us; time has left its traces, we find them aged. Happy, indeed, if there be no vacant place by the hearth!

A winter morning in our northern clime is dreary enough, particularly when one's brain is full of pictures of the sunlit tropics. Very dreary is the colourless daylight, the dull and rayless sky, the cold—which one had forgotten, the old trees—now bare, the dripping, moss-grown lime-trees, the ivy on the grey stones.

And yet how good it is to be at home! What joy to see them all again, including the old servants who watched over my infancy; to return to the sweet, forgotten habits, the pleasant winter evenings as of old; and how strange a dream does Oceania seem as I sit by the fire!

That morning when I came home to Brightbury, the road was strewn with luggage, parcels and packing-cases. To unpack all these is one of the amusements of home-coming. Savage weapons, Maori idols, head-dresses of Polynesian chiefs, shells and corals, looking grotesque indeed as they came to the light of day again in our old house, under the sky of England. I was especially and deeply touched as I unpacked the dried flowers and the withered garlands, which still preserved their exotic perfume and made my room redolent of Oceanian odours.

III

Some days after this a letter reached me covered with American post-marks, and delivered at last by overland mail. The address was in the writing of my friend George T., of Papeete, known to the Tahitians as Tatehau. Within, I found two sheets in Rarahu's large and laboured hand—her cry of woe across the seas.

RARAHU TO LOTI

Papéuriri, 15 Tannaré, 1874.

Papéuriri, January 15, 1874.

E hoa íno, e Loti iti,

Dear friend, O my little Loti,

e ta ú tane iti here,

O my dear little husband,

e ta ú manao raa i Tahiti nei;

O thou, my only thought in Tahiti;

ia ora na óe i te Atua mau.

I salute thee by the true God.

Teie taú parau iti ia óe te rahi nei toú peápeá ía óc

This letter will tell you of my sadness for you.

Mai te mahana e reva tu ai óe ra,

Since the day when you went away,

aita ia e faito i tou nei mauiui e tau

nothing can give the measure of my grief.

Aita roa tu i moe naae tou manao ia oe mai to óe reva raa

Never has my thought forgotten you since you went away.

Aue taua iti e, teie te tahi parau iti :

O my dear friend, this is my word :

eiaha pai oe e manao
e faa ipoipo vau i te tane;

e aha vau e faa ipoipo
i tetane, no te mea o oe
iho te tane o vau

A hoi mai pai ei parahi
taua i tau fenua i Bora-
Bora, ei haapaa i nia iho
i tau fenua i Bora-
Bora—

Eiaha pai oe e haa-
maori to oe na fenua,
eiaha atoa oe e hamani
ino mai ia ú

Teie atoa te tahi par-
au iti; a hoi mai pai oe i
Bora-Bora; no atu ia ore
ta oe taoa, aita vau i nounou rahi, eiaha pai oe e
haapao ite reira, e ia hoi
mai oe i Tahiti nei.

Aue! tou mauruuru ia
a apiti taua iti e.

Aue te oaoa o tau
mafatu ia farerei faahou
taua iti e te ia oe, tou
manao, e tau arofa ite
mau mahana atoa.

Aue taua iti a tau
manao raa ia oe ei tane
iti na ú,

Aue tou nounou i to
oe tino iti hia amu rahi
no oe! . . .

Teie te tahi parau no
tau parahi raa i Papéu-
riri nei!

Do not think that I
shall ever marry.

How could I ever
marry since you are my
husband?

Come back that we may
dwell together in my land
of Bora-Bora, and settle
in my land of Bora-Bora.

Do not stay so long in
your own land, and be
faithful to me.

Here is another word;
come back to Bora-Bora.
It does not matter that
you are not rich.   I do
not want much; do not
let that trouble you, and
came back to Tahiti.

Ah what joy to be to-
gether!

Ah what joy to my
heart to be with you once
more, my thought and my
love of every day!

Ah that dear thought
that you are my husband!

Oh, I wish I had you
here to eat you up!

Here is a word about
my stay at Papéouriri.

Aita vau i taiata, te parahi noa nei au mai.	I am good, I keep very quiet,
Te faaea maitai noa neia vau io Tiahoui-va-hine,	I rest well in the home of Tiahoui, the wife.
te ore ae faaea i te hamani maitai mai ia vau—	She does not cease to be kind to me.
E tau hoa iti oto rahi e, te faaite atu nei au i tau nei parau hopea ia oe, aita roa tu vau e maitai noa e i teie nei, na tui faahou hia vau i te mai rahi ta oe i ite l nia ia u a faaea i tua ra, hoe a huru mai, aita e huru e;	Oh my great grief, I let you know to end this letter that I am never well now; I have fallen again into the sickness which you could cure me of; the same sickness and not another.
e i teie nei ra pohe raa, na roto noa vau ite faaoromai, no te mea ua moe e atu na oe; ahiri hoi oe l pihaiho ia ù, e mama rii oe ia vau nei…	And I endure it with patience because you have forgotten me; if you were with me you would ease me a little.
I teie nei ra, te tuu atu nei o Tiahoui ma i to raua aroha ia oe, e te fetii rii atoa a oia toa-hai o vau nei;	And now Tiahoui and her people remind you of their friendship for you, and her parents, and I also.
aita roatu oe iti e moe noae i te mau taata no tau fenua iti ia ai te fara.	Never will you be for-gotten by the men of my country.
Tirara parau.	I have finished my words.
Ia ora na oe, tau tane iti here.	I greet you, my dear little husband.
Ia ora na o Loti iti.	I greet you, O my Loti.

Na Rarahu ta oe va-
hine iti

From Rarahu your
little wife.

Rarahu.

Rarahu.

Ua horoa hia eau teie nei parau ia Tatehau ma-taiore, aita pai au iteite ioa o to oe fenua e nana e papai.

I have given this letter to Tatehau (rat's-eye), I do not quite know the name of the place where I should write to you.

Ia ora na oe, tau here iti

I greet you, my dearest friend,

Rarahu.

Rarahu.

IV.

NOTE BY PLUNKET.

Loti wrote a long letter to Rarahu in which he expressed in the Tahitian tongue his great love for his little friend.   He told her, in such a way as she could find intelligible, by particular expressions and figures of speech, of his six months' voyage in the *Reindeer,* of the storm off Cape Horn which had put the vessel in danger and had swept many of his cases full of treasures into the sea.

Then he told her of his return home, of his native land, and of his mother, saying that, in spite of all these much-loved things, he dreamed of seeing the great ocean once more and returning to the dear island and his little savage wife.

V

RARAHU TO LOTI, A YEAR LATER

Papeete, te 3 no Tetepa 1874.

E tau hoa iti here rahi, e tau mea iti mauiui rahi, ia ora na oe i te Atua mau.

E maere rahi roa ino au ta oe rata i te ore et ae mai ia u nei, no te mea a pae ae nei tau rata i papai atu na e aita roa tu et ahi parau iti api i tae noa mai nei no oe.

E riro ra paha oe aita oe e haamanao faahou mai ia u, inaha te hio nei mau rata e hapono atu ia oe, aita roa tu oe e poroi noa mai.

Hoa iti mauiui rahi e, no te aha oe na moe raa tu ia u?

Aita roa tu vau nei e maitai noa e; te pohe, te mai. . .

Ahiri hoi oe e papai rii noa mai ia u, e mahana-hana e ia tau nei aau, aita roa tu ra hoi oe e manao naa e i te reira ra huru.

Area ra vau nei, te vai noa nei a ia tau roha ia oe, e tau atoa hoi ai rahi

Papeete, December 3rd, 1874.

O my dear little friend, O dear object of my grief, I greet you by the true God.

I am grievously surprised at receiving no letter from you, because I have written to you five times and not a word from you has ever reached me.

Perhaps it has happened that you no longer remember me; I see that my letters were sent to you and you have never told me of it.

Dear object of my grief, why do you forget me?

Never shall I be well again now, the sickness, the pain. . .

But if you were to write to me a little, it would warm my heart, but you never think of that.

As for me, my love for you is still the same, and likewise my tears for you;

ia oe; mai te mea e te vai na e a te hoe maa aroha iti roto ia oe no u, na oe iho ia o manao mai.

Ahiri au e maitai ia haere atu a pihai iho ia oe, ua reva e atu na ia vau, aita ra hoi tau ravea e tae atu ai au....

— Teie te tahi parau i Papeete nei: I te avae i mua e te oroa rahi i Papeete, ei te mootua tamahine no te arii vahine.

Ua te oroa nehenehe roa, e ua úpaúpa te mau vahine e tae mai te poipoi—

Ua úpaúpa nau atou; ei nia i tau upoo a tahi hei huruhuru manu— tau mafatu ra merahi pea-pea...

E i teie nei ra, o Pomare arii ma, e to na mootua tamahine iti Pomare, e o Ariitea, parau ia oe: ia ora na.

Aita roa tu e parau rii api i Tahiti nei, maori ra e, o Ariifaite te tane o te arii vahine, ua pohe roa ino ia i roto i Atete nei i te ono...

. . . .

. . . .

Aita roa tu mea mai-

and so if a little love were left in your heart for me you yourself would think of me.

If I could have gone far to meet you I should have gone, but my plan could not be carried out.

Here is a word about Papeete: There was a grand fête at Papeete last month, for the queen's granddaughter.

And it was very grand, and the women danced till the morning.

And I was there too; I had a crown of birds' feathers on my head, but my heart was very sad—

And now the Queen Pomaré and her family and her granddaughter Pomaré and Ariitéa say they greet you.

Never any news in Tahiti, excepting that Ariefaité, the queen's husband, died on the sixth of the month of August.

. . . .

. . . .

Never again will my

tai nou merahi aroha no oe, te tane iti nou! . . .

great love for you, my husband, be satisfied!

. . . .

Aue! Aue! hoi te tiare iti tarona iti e ua maheahea i teie nei! . . .

Alas! Alas! the little arum flower, too, is faded now!

. . . .

Ia mua ta iho te tiare iti tarona menehenehe!

I teienei ua mahehea, aita merahi menehenehe!

Before becoming like this the little arum flower was pretty!

Now it is faded, it is no longer pretty!

. . . .

Ahiri tou e pere rau manu, e reva vau maoro i nia i te tara no Paea, ei aore te hoe iti ae e hio ia ù. . . .

Aue! Aue! e tau tane here e, e ta taio aroha rahi! . . . Aue! Aue! hoi taua iti e! . . .

Tirara parau.

Ia ora na oe i te Atua mau.

Na Rarahu.

If I had the wings of a bird I would fly far away to the top of Paea, so that no one should see me more.

Alas! Alas! O my dear husband, O my well-beloved friend. Alas! Alas! my dear friend!

I have ended my words.

I greet you in the true God.

Rarahu.

VI

LOTI'S DIARY

London, February 20th, 1875.

I was walking down Regent Street at nine in the evening. The night was raw and foggy; thousands of gas-lamps lighted the human ant-hill,—the black and dripping crowd. Behind me a voice cried: "Ia ora na, Loti!"

I turned round in great surprise and recognized my friend George T——., the man called by the Tahitians Tatehau, whom I had left in Tahiti, bent on ending his days there.

VII

When we were comfortably seated in the chimney corner we began talking of the delicious island.

"Rarahu," he said, a little embarrassed— "Yes, I think she was well when I left the country; indeed, if I had taken leave of her she would most probably have given me some messages for you. As you know she left Papeete when you did, and it was said in the country that Loti and Rarahu could not bear to part and had gone together to Europe. No one knew but I that she was with her friend Tiahoui; I, who received her letters with no other address than *"to Tatehau Rat's-eye; to forward to Loti."*— When she came back to Papeete six or eight months later, she was prettier than ever; more of a woman and more fully formed. Her great sadness gave her added charm; she had the grace of an elegy.

"She went to live with a young French officer, whose passion for her was quite out of the common; he was jealous even of your memory. She was still known as Loti's little wife.—He had solemnly sworn that he would take her back to France with him.

"This lasted two or three months, and during

that time she was the most elegant and remarkable-looking woman in Papeete. At the end of that time an event took place which had long been expected. Little Pomaré V. flickered out of life one night, only a few days after a grand fête given for her entertainment, and of which she had drawn up the programme. The old queen was so overwhelmed with grief at this last and cruelest blow that she will probably not long survive it.* She has retired meanwhile into a lonely dwelling built close to the little girl's grave, and refused to see any living soul.

" At that time Rarahu followed the fashion of court attendants, and in sign of mourning cut her magnificent black hair quite short. The queen was touched by her devotion, but it gave rise to a quarrel between Rarahu and her lover; and as, in fact, she did not care for him, she made it a reason for parting from him.

" I wish I could tell you that she had gone back to live with her friend at Papéouriri. But unfortunately the poor little thing remained at Papeete, where at this day I fear she is leading a wholly dissolute life."

VIII

NOTE BY PLUNKET

From this time forward Loti's diaries only very rarely contain any trace of the reminiscences he

---

* Queen Pomaré died in 1877, leaving the throne to her second son Ariiaue. She had survived her little granddaughter about two years. From the day of her death may be reckoned the beginning of the end of Tahiti, from the point of view of native customs, local colour and the charm of individuality.

treasured in his heart of the distant Polynesian island;—the image of Rarahu grows more remote, and fades away. These fragments are mixed up with the adventures of a life of wild excitement and no small eccentricity, in many and various lands, chiefly in Africa and afterwards in Italy.

FRAGMENTS OF LOTI'S DIARIES

Sierra Leone, March, 1875.

Oh, my best-beloved little friend, shall we ever meet again in that distant land—in our dear little island—seated in the dusk on the coral shore.

.　　.　　.　　.　　.　　.　　.　　.　　.　　.　　.

Bobdiarah, Senegambia, October, 1875.

This is the rainy season, out there; the season when the earth is carpeted with pink flowers like our English snowdrops;—the mosses are wet and the woods full of water. Here the sun is setting, blood-stained and lurid, over desert stretches of sand; out there it is three in the morning, quite dark, and *toupapahous* are prowling in the woods.

Two years lie over those days—and I love that land as I did in the early time there. The impression it has left is permanent; as deep as that of Bright-bury, of my native home, while so many more recent ones have died out. My little hut, nestling at the feet of the great palms—and my little savage wife!

Good God! shall I never see them again; shall I never again hear the wailing pipe of the *vivo*, after sunset, under the coco-trees on the strand?

.   .   .   .

Southampton, March, 1876.

Tahiti—Bora-Bora—Oceania.—How far, how very far away it all is, good Heavens!

Shall I ever go back there; and if I did, what now should I find there; what but bitter disenchantment and poignant regrets for the past?

I weep as I remember the lost charm of those first years, the charm which no power can restore—all the things which I have no power even to record on paper, and which are already dim and fading in my memory.

Alas! Where now are the delights of Tahiti? The queen's fêtes, the *himénés* in the moonlight, Rarahu, Ariitéa, Taìmaha, where are they? That terrible night in Moorea, all my emotions and dreams of that past time—what has become of them all? And that well-beloved brother John, who shared with me all these first youthful impressions, thrilling, strange and enchanting as they were? That heady fragrance of gardenias—the murmur of the high wind on the coral reefs—the mysterious shadows and hoarse voices of the night—the wild breeze which swept over us in the darkness. . . . Where is all the indefinable charm of that land, where the freshness of the impressions we shared and of our joys in common?

For me, alas! there is a heart-rending pleasure in going back to those memories which time is bearing away, whenever some accident revives them; a page I wrote there, a dried flower, a *reva-reva*, a scent of Tahiti still preserved by hapless wreaths now crumbling into dust, or a word of that soft melancholy tongue, the outlandish language which I am fast forgetting.

Here, at Southampton, we lead a life of routine in mess-rooms and smoking-rooms; we lodge where we can and make friends with whom we may; meeting we know not wherefor, and drowning thought as chance may direct.

I have changed greatly within these two years, and as I look back I do not know myself. I have flung myself since into a life of pleasure and folly; it seems to me the only logical way of taking an existence I never desired, and of which the aim and end are to me an insoluble problem.

.   .   .   .

IX

Malta, May 2nd, 1876.

Forty or more of us, officers of the British navy, were sitting in a café in Valetta, in the island of Malta. Our squadron had put into port here for a few days, on the way to the Levant, where the French and German consuls had just been murdered, and where grave complications seemed likely to occur. Among the party I had come across an officer who, like myself, had lived in Oceania, and we had withdrawn a little from the rest, to talk over our Tahitian experiences.

X

" You were speaking just now of little Rarahu of Bora-Bora," said Lieutenant Benson, coming up to us. He had been in Tahiti later than either of us. " She had fallen very low in these latter days—but she was a strange little creature. Wreaths of flowers, always fresh, on a death's-head face.—At last she had no home of her own, and wherever she went she dragged an old cat at her heels, a feeble thing with rings in its ears, to which she was devoted. This cat followed her everywhere with lamentable mewings. She often slept under the queen's roof, for in spite of everything Pomaré still showed her the greatest pity and kindness.

" She was dying of consumption, and as she had taken to drinking brandy the course of the disease was rapid.

" One day, in November, 1875—she may have been about eighteen—we heard she had set out with her infirm old cat for her native island of Bora-Bora, where she had gone to die, and where, as it would seem, she lived only a few days."

XI

I felt a mortal chill about my heart, a mist floated before my eyes.

My poor little savage friend!—Often when I awoke in the night I still seemed to see her; in spite of everything her image rose before me with its indescribable, sweet sadness; and with a vague hope, vague notions of forgiveness and redemption—and all was at an end, sunk in the mire, lost in the gulf of eternal destruction.

There was a deadly chill about my heart; and a mist floated before my eyes; and there I sat motionless;—and we went on discussing our reminiscences of Oceania.

I, too, under the gay blaze of lamps reflected from the mirrors, in the midst of the cheerful clatter of talk, laughter, British toasts and clinking of glasses —I, too, took my part in the general concert of commonplace and foolishness. Like the rest, I could say in an airy tone:

" A lovely land is Oceania!—Beautiful creatures those Tahitian women;—not classically Greek as to features, but with a beauty of their own which is even more attractive, and antique figures and limbs! Mentally, incomplete creatures whom one loves like fine fruit or fresh waters and gorgeous flowers.

" As I saw Tahiti, through the enchanting prism of extreme youth, it was too delicious, too strange. ... In short it is a delightful land when one is but twenty; but one soon gets tired of it, and perhaps it is as well not to go back after one has turned thirty."

. . . .

XII

But at night, when I was alone again in silence and darkness, a gloomy dream weighed on my soul, a vision born neither of sleep nor wakefulness—one of those phantoms which fold their bats' wings to settle on a sick man's pillow, or to squat on the panting heart of a criminal.

. . . .

NATUAEA

(A dim vision of the night.)

Over there, the other way up, far, far from Europe, the great hill of Bora-Bora uplifted its awful shape in the twilight grey of dream-light.

I was nearing it on board a black bark which glided noiselessly over a stagnant sea, driven by no wind yet speeding on. Quite, quite close to the shore, under overhanging black masses which seemed to be tall trees, the vessel grounded on coral and stopped. It was night in my dream, and I lay still waiting for the day, my eyes fixed on the land in undefinable horror. At last the sun rose, a huge pale sun—so pale that it might have been for a sign from heaven announcing to man the end of the ages —a sinister meteor, heralding final chaos—a huge, dead sun.

Bora-Bora was visible in the wan light; then I discerned human figures seated, and seeeming to expect me, and I got out on the beach. Among the trunks of the coco-palms, under that high and melancholy grey colonnade, women were huddled on the ground, their heads resting on their hands as though keeping a funeral wake; they seemed to have sat there from all time; their long hair covered them almost entirely, and they were motionless; their eyes were shut, but through the transparent lids I was aware of their gaze fixed on me.

In their midst lay a human figure, white and stark, stretched on a bed of pandanus. I went up to this sleeping phantom, I bent over the dead face— Rarahu laughed aloud.—At this ghostly laughter the sun went out in the sky, and I was in the dark once more.

Then a great wind swept through the air and I was confusedly conscious of horrible things;—the tall palms, wrung by mysterious gusts—tattooed spectres squatting in their shade—Maori grave-yards, in that strange soil which turns bones red— weird sounds of the sea and coral shore, the blue crabs which love the dead swarming in the darkness —and amid all Rarahu laid out, her childlike body shrouded in her long back hair—Rarahu, with hollow eyes, and laughing that eternal laugh—the soulless laugh of the Toupapahous. . . .

" O my dear little friend, O my fragrant flower of evening! My heart is very sick since I can see you no more. O my star of the morning, my eyes melt into tears because you do not return! I greet you by the true God, in the Christian faith.

" Your little friend,

" RARAHU."

THE END.